The Modern Fairies

Also by Clare Pollard

Novel
Delphi

Children's novel
The Untameables

Poetry
The Heavy-Petting Zoo
Bedtime
Look, Clare! Look!
Changeling
Ovid's Heroines
Incarnation

Non-fiction
Fierce Bad Rabbits

Play
The Weather

The Modern Fairies

CLARE POLLARD

FIG TREE
an imprint of
PENGUIN BOOKS

FIG TREE

UK | USA | Canada | Ireland | Australia
India | New Zealand | South Africa

Fig Tree is part of the Penguin Random House group of companies
whose addresses can be found at global.penguinrandomhouse.com.

First published 2024
001

Copyright © Clare Pollard, 2024

The moral right of the author has been asserted

Set in 13.5/16pt Garamond MT Std
Typeset by Jouve (UK), Milton Keynes
Printed and bound in Great Britain by Clays Ltd, Elcograf S.p.A.

The authorized representative in the EEA is Penguin Random House Ireland,
Morrison Chambers, 32 Nassau Street, Dublin D02 YH68

A CIP catalogue record for this book is available from the British Library

ISBN: 978-0-241-67245-7

www.greenpenguin.co.uk

MIX
Paper | Supporting
responsible forestry
FSC® C018179

Penguin Random House is committed to a
sustainable future for our business, our readers
and our planet. This book is made from Forest
Stewardship Council® certified paper.

To my husband

The histories that will be written about this court after we are gone will be better and more entertaining than any novel, and I fear that those who come after us will not be able to believe them, but will think that they are just fairy tales.

– The Duchesse d'Orléans

Cast of Characters

During the reign of Louis XIV (1643–1715) many people shared the same first names, so the names I use consistently are in capitals.

MADAME MARIE-Catherine D'AULNOY
   JUDITH, her mother
   NICOLAS, her father
   BARON D'AULNOY, her husband, separated
   Charles BONENFANT, her lover, deceased
   JUDITH, daughter
   THÉRÈSE, daughter
   FRANÇOISE, daughter
   BELLE-BELLE, a marmoset
   MIMI, nurse
   ANNE, cook
   BERTHE, housemaid

At the salon

CHARLES PERRAULT
   Marie Perrault, his wife, deceased
   Charles, son
   Pierre, son

Madame Marie-Jeanne L'Héritier de Villandon, known as TÉLÉSILLE, Perrault's cousin

MADAME HENRIETTE-Julie DE MURAT
  COUNT DE MURAT, her husband

MADAME ANGÉLIQUE TIQUET
  CLAUDE, her husband
  MOURA, her valet
  MADAME MIAOU, her cat

Charles BRIOU
CHARLOTTE-ROSE Caumont de La Force, lady-in-waiting for the Dauphine
Marie Anne de Bourbon, known as the PRINCESSE DE CONTI, Louis and Athénaïs's legitimized daughter

ABBÉ Charles COTIN
Charles de SAINT-ÉVREMOND

At the court

KING LOUIS XIV
Madame de Montespan, known as ATHÉNAÏS, the king's official mistress
MADAME DE MAINTENON, the king's new mistress
Jean-Baptiste COLBERT, controller of general finances
Maria Anna Christina Victoria of Bavaria, known as THE DAUPHINE
FAGON, the doctor
LA VOISIN, a fortune teller
Gabriel Nicolas de La REYNIE, chief of police

Contents

1. The Tale of Donkey-Skin, Part One

'There was once an omnipotent king. Perhaps, some said, the most powerful ruler there had ever been. They said too – of course they did – that he managed to be both just in peacetime, and in wartime utterly terrifying. His subjects were completely content, whilst his enemies shuddered with fear. And this king had – of course he had – the most charming and beautiful wife imaginable, and their little girl was the most darling little doll. Really, one might say that their lives were perfect.'

So Charles Perrault begins to tell the tale of 'Donkey-Skin'. So, too, we begin our story.

In Madame d'Aulnoy's salon, Perrault's small audience sit forward keenly in their seats to hear what inevitable disaster will strike this faultless family. For the energy that lies behind all stories is a destructive energy – the urge to burn down what *is* for what *might be*. It is late autumn in the late seventeenth century, in the time of the reign of Louis XIV. The gathering is in a fine room on the Rue Saint-Benoît, in Paris, snugly luxurious with heavy, embroidered coral-coloured brocade; candles dance close to every hem.

Earlier, Charles Perrault was introduced to various members of the elite, intellectual crowd who have been meeting here regularly, for the purpose of sharing what at this time are still largely known as Mother Goose tales – although some know them as tales of the stork, or even Donkey-Skin tales. Or perhaps you know them by the newer name, contes de fées or fairy tales? Well, it is Madame d'Aulnoy herself who has coined this term, and in the process made quite a craze of them.

Though Charles is usually good at people's names, scanning around again he realizes a couple have slipped his mind already. There is his cousin, Marie-Jeanne L'Héritier de Villandon, ardent and a touch pious – who he cannot help but like, though he is also slightly wary of the manner in which her ordinary face so shines with good intentions. His cousin is his point of entry into this circle, thinking to be the one to lift his present gloom. She has asked that he call her Télésille within this context – it has become the fashion to have a salon name, and hers is after a Greek poet who led women into battle, something that he finds mildly preposterous but is trying to remember in politeness.

Looking around, he can also see one of the king's illegitimate daughters, the Princesse de Conti, who always sits forward with the easy casualness of wealth, as though her legs are open beneath her skirts. A clear-skinned blonde with a strong jaw, she wears no wig or make-up. Is attractive, but in the manner of a dashing young prince rather than a princess – she smokes tobacco rakishly from a pipe.

Wealthy heiress Madame Angélique Tiquet he recognizes at once – she sprawls louchely in the soft chair at the left, wearing a pink shepherdess's frock rummaged out of the salon's fancy-dress box (having acted along to an earlier tale), and is still holding her crook like a sceptre. Angélique Tiquet is the sort of woman who spills from every dress that she wears despite her age; sugar crystals bedeck the corners of her sumptuous mouth, with its rotten front tooth. She has a white cat with a jewelled collar that she often carries under her arm.

There, too, is a rare man who has been allowed into the circle – Abbé Cotin, a mediocre clergyman and scribbler known for his tedious sonnets. Beside him, her narrow nose flaring at the abbé's mere presence, is sharp-tongued Madame Henriette de Murat. Then pretty, posy Charlotte-Rose Caumont ... de La something – Force, that was it – in the latest fashions, who he recognizes as a lady-in-waiting from the court. The others, though. Minor aristocrats. Who is that tall young man with long lashes?

Thick hot chocolate is being served in very beautiful china with a pale green glaze. Women carefully check their teeth and upper lips with their tongues after each sip, for tidemarks.

This is Perrault's first time at the salon, and he means to charm, for his cousin's sake as well as his own. The tale of 'Donkey-Skin' – 'Peau d'Ane' – is one that has always delighted him, since his nurse told it to him by the fire's embers. As one of the esteemed forty members of the Académie Française, that council pertaining to the French language, known as 'les immortels' after the academy's motto 'À l'immortalité' ('To Immortality'), he thinks he knows how to woo a small, literary audience such as this – the tale must be brief and sparkling:

a glass of champagne you have finished before you even realize it's in your hand.

Those who take a moment to admire Perrault see a man in his fifties, under a brown wig that puts one in mind of a handsome spaniel. It is often said that he has grown into his face, which is open, with lucent eyes that cannot help but tend towards merry. He is one of those men of the world with real charisma, who have the great gift of being interested in everyone, from the Dauphin to the cook. To be held in his attention for a few gleaming moments is usually to like him, an effect which he internally, humbly acknowledges.

'Imagine their magnificent palace!' he continues. 'Courtiers from all around the globe come to see their paintings by Rubens and Leonardo, their statues by Bernini, their lavish hall of mirrors . . .' This raises another chuckle, the audience aware that he is describing the Galerie des Glaces in Louis XIV's magnificent palace at Versailles, one of the wonders of the Western world – the room Charles Perrault himself furnished with over three hundred large mirrors. Perhaps the most famous room in France, it is an Aladdin's cave crowded with flatteringly lit beauties, gazing at versions upon versions of themselves. But in acknowledging it, Perrault means also to acknowledge what everyone here surely knows – that since his friend Colbert's death he has fallen out of favour with Louis XIV. He doesn't want anyone to think they must tiptoe around him on the subject of Versailles. He still has a pension after all; is proud of what he achieved there. It is no shame to move on.

Perrault makes sure of eye contact with Madame d'Aulnoy as he speaks, hoping to delight his hostess most of all. He was impressed by her recent novel, the society sensation *The Story of Hypolitus, Count of Douglas*, so is keen to get to know the writer behind it – although there is something cool and slippery about her gaze. For a moment, Perrault pictures a turret with glass walls and himself as a knight-errant, struggling slightly to catch his footing. It is not a feeling he is very familiar with. He is trying to establish a playful tone, but he realizes that it feels new and unnerving to him, to be encouraged to talk lightly of kings and palaces this way. Is this why they tell fairy tales in here? To slip rebellious thoughts past the censors, in the guise of nursery stories?

But all verbal storytelling is a kind of improvisation, done on nerve, and his instincts tell him that he must get on with the plot. 'The king's stables boasted steeds of every description,' Perrault continues. 'But something shocked those who entered the stables, though they hardly dared talk of it – the place of honour was held by a hideous donkey with two enormous ears, that had earned its position by shitting golden coins each morning instead of dung.'

A laugh at this, which is an easy laugh, he knows. His cousin Télésille's eyes gleam with a curious mixture of emotions – he imagines she is swallowing her private distaste for such humour, but also still trusts his ability to beguile a room.

'Now God, who keeps us attentive by mingling good with evil, permitted the queen to sicken. She grew pale and thin; her eyes glittered. Neither the learned physicians nor the charlatans could stop her fever. Finally, with her last breath, the queen said to her husband, "Promise me that you will only marry again if you find a woman cleverer and more beautiful than me." She was confident, you see – in her calculated vanity – that it would be impossible to find such a woman, so this dying wish would prohibit her husband from remarriage. We must admit that as she expired, she felt rather smug, with no inkling at all of the terrible consequences she had set in motion. "Of course, my love, anything for you," the king sobbed as she died in his arms.'

(Charles swallows the saliva that lacquers his own tongue. He will not think of it now, in public. He will not think of it.)

'For a few months, the king was inconsolable, but then urged by his courtiers to secure an heir, he did agree to marry again. This was not an easy matter, though, for he was determined to keep his promise, and who could possibly equal his queen in intelligence and beauty? Only his daughter, who every day charmed him more, with her slender grace and her sky-blue eyes. Only his daughter.

'The thought turned in his head; it twisted his guts. It began to possess him. Only his daughter. She was his wife in miniature, his wife come back. The answer to the riddle. Only by marrying his daughter could he fulfil his vow to his dying wife! And so, one day, as she played by his feet, he proposed to her. The princess laughed, as at a game, but then she realized it was not a game. "Don't frighten me, Father."

'"It's what your mother wanted. Her dying wish."

'"Please don't talk so strangely," the princess replied, shivering as though a shadow had moved over her.

'Deeply troubled at this turn of events, the princess sought out her fairy godmother who lived in a grotto of' – Perrault glances round the room at the rich, coral fabrics and shimmering candelabras and improvises here – 'coral and pearls.'

Perrault's audience, largely female, nod appreciatively, their pale wigs bobbing in unison like a flock of doves thrown seed. They seem to agree that this is the type of place where fairy godmothers are found. There is the sound of drinks being slurped, a cup skittering upon a saucer, the fire's steady crackle. The fire is a touch too hot, so Perrault is gilded with sweat, though he surely can't be nervous. Often, when public speaking, he has quelled his nerves with the technique of picturing the audience naked, but in this instance – amongst so many of the female species – he feels that it would only increase his perspiration.

He opens his mouth again. '"I know why you're here," the fairy godmother said. "Your heart is heavy. But we godmothers have our wiles. I'm sure nothing can harm you if you follow my advice. Tell him that first you must have a dress which has the exact colour of the sky. It will be impossible." So the young princess went, aquiver, to her father. But the moment he heard her request, he summoned his best tailors and ordered them to make a dress the colour of the sky, straight away, or he'd hang them all. The following day the princess got her dress. It was the changeable, radiant blue of Heaven.

'Next, her godmother advised: "Ask for a dress the precise colour of the moon. Surely that really is impossible." But almost anything, you see, is possible when you're the most powerful ruler there has ever been in the entire world. The king summoned his embroiderers, made threats, and four days later a dress the colour of moonlight was ready – placed in the dark of the wardrobe, it even emitted a ghostly glow.

'"All right," said the godmother, looking a little more anxious this time. "Let's have one more try – a dress as radiant as the sun. What are they going to do, set it on fire?" This time the king summoned his jeweller and ordered him to make a cloth of gold and jewels, warning him that if he failed, he'd be beheaded. Within a week the jeweller had a finished dress that so dazzled the eyes it left little floating dots on the retinas of everyone who saw it.'

Perrault likes this bit of the tale – the pattern of it. The rhythm. He likes the shapes things make. And he likes beautiful, refined things: frescos, hyacinths, clockmakers, marzipans, butterfly wings, golden tableware, fountains, good shoes, the nightingale's song. He is an aesthetic man. For all his disappointment, in the end, at the court of Versailles, he tries to be proud of what he helped to create there – civilization.

The room listens intently – he has them caught – as he continues his tale: 'The princess knew she was expected to thank the king, but the word stuck in her throat. Once again, her godmother hissed advice in her ear: "I've got it! Ask him for a cloak made of the skin of that donkey in the royal stable. He loves that donkey. There's no way he'll kill it, unless I'm badly mistaken."

'This was her best idea so far, but she did not understand how the king's desire to bed his daughter now overwhelmed every other consideration. He was tortured by longing, a sensation that – given his position – he had never experienced before. Almost immediately, he spat out the command. Minutes later, his donkey's still-warm skin was laid before the princess: bloodied, stupid-eared, buck-toothed, wet-eyed. "Enough now, child," he said. "We wed tomorrow."

'Now both the princess and her godmother were truly terrified. The godmother decided the only option was for the princess to escape, disguised beneath the donkey-skin. She filled a chest with the princess's clothes, powders, mirror and jewels, and gave her a magic wand, telling her to touch it to the ground when she wanted the chest to appear. But otherwise the girl was on her own. So, on the morning she was meant to marry her father, the princess vanished.'

When Perrault says this a sudden cold feeling comes over him. He finds he doesn't glance up at Madame d'Aulnoy, because he remembers – how could he be so foolish as to have picked this tale for his debut? – that this is, in part, her story. He recalls, now, how when she reappeared in the city a few years ago and opened a salon, the halls of Versailles were abuzz.

Gossip has it that Madame d'Aulnoy was married off

by her father to Baron d'Aulnoy when she was just a little girl, for financial motives. The baron was not a real baron of course, but a drunken libertine who had purchased the title. And then, after years of rumours that he ill-used and degraded his young wife (and after she had lost two of her three babies, poor thing), he was imprisoned in the Bastille for treason, having vocally complained about the king's taxation system.

But then – this was the twist in the tale – the baron was released. Rumour swirls that this was because, having been framed for the crime, he had finally proven his innocence. It had all been a conspiracy by Madame d'Aulnoy, her mother and two men (assumed to be their lovers) to falsely accuse him! The two men had their heads chopped off, whilst Madame d'Aulnoy herself was jailed in a tower with her third, newborn baby, only to escape by jumping from a window.

Did Madame d'Aulnoy flee in disguise like Donkey-Skin? And the question which obsesses the court, naturally, also resurfaces now in Perrault's mind – why, all these years later, is she allowed to be here in Paris, at the heart of this salon?

2. The Tale of the Good Girl

You must excuse me – how wrong of me not to begin at the beginning, which is to say with birth. Stories are about people and their characters – their development, circumstances, complex web of relationships, their behaviour and its consequences, their interactions with luck – and the true beginning of character is birth, as its true end is death. Oh, if you wish it later, we can choose not to end with that, but we must at least acknowledge, as adults, that such an ending is a turning-away. And this fairy tale, I warn you, is very much for grown-ups.

Let us begin with a birth, then. This is a time when childbirth is generally fraught, and many women die of it. Some are too young, married off at twelve or thirteen; some in their late forties and squeezing out a sickly, four-teenth child; some simply unlucky. They die of bleeding, often, life draining and puddling until there is not enough liquid left in their veins to push through their hearts, or from infection, or from doctors, who in this period know next to nothing but are paid well, largely to reassure men like themselves that nothing further could have been done, which makes it very dangerous to see one sweep into your room in their black robes.

Madame d'Aulnoy, though, who is not of course born a madame – how absurd such titles seem when we apply them to those tiny sightless, shitting creatures that are human babies – but a little Marie-Catherine, is pushed incrementally out on to a bed in Normandy in 1652: her indigo skull slimed with curds, scarlet petals falling quickly on the sheets from a perineal tear, her mother's rancid screams blotting out the bells of the medieval church and the rushing river and shivering apple trees.

Marie is the first child of Nicolas and Judith, and the birth is long and hard, her mother's young body not yet slackened by time. For Judith, an ambitious woman who likes politics, flirting, languages and the opera, it is the worst day of her life – an unjust punishment that makes her petulant and sullen for months afterwards – but luckily there are no complications and the doctors do not come with their unclean implements and jars of leeches. Nicolas is told it is a girl, and kicks a washstand, cursing his fate as is customary.

Judith has absolutely zero interest in suckling a child – the very idea of it she finds grimly bovine – so, as was common, the baby is handed straight to a nurse, Mimi (whose own son was stillborn, fortuitously for them). Marie clambers blindly to the ridged, pink-brown nipple to worry out a pearl of sweet human milk. 'Good girl,' Mimi coos, gently – tender memories pooling in her head and breasts and eyes. Mimi appears to be the platonic ideal of a wet nurse: slow-moving, heavy, mild. 'Oh! She's such a good little girl.'

Marie continues to be a good girl as she grows older. She knows, for example, to steer clear of her father when he is drinking red wine, which aggravates his self-pity – amongst his many woes he is useless at billiards and suffers painful attacks of gout, tiny crystals accruing in his joints – and makes him prone to see his daughter, suddenly, as a tiny jangling memento mori; a skeleton in a little girl's dress come to lead him by the hand to the abyss. She knows when to pat her mother gently on the back during a crying jag, and say *there there*, but also never to bore her with playthings or tiresome questions, for Judith has decided that there is nothing more tedious for an intelligent woman than her own baby.

Mimi, her nurse, turns out to be the little girl's salvation, sensual and naturally maternal, always tickling the cat's belly or letting it gnaw her knuckle, wiping Marie's face clean with spittle or fussing over her hair. Sometimes her hugs give Marie a claustrophobic feeling, but it is better than her mother's reeling distance. Mimi calls Marie 'ma puce'– my flea; 'mon coco' – my egg; or 'ma petite crotte' – my little poo.

In front of the fire at night, as she combs Marie's locks, she tells her folk stories, like that of Little Thumb – the delicate, quiet boy born no bigger than a thumb who is taken for stupid. Mimi tells of a great famine, during which Little Thumb's father and mother decide they cannot bear to see their children die of hunger, so will abandon them in the wood. Of how Little Thumb leaves a trail of pebbles the first time and finds his way back, but then, when his parents try to abandon him again, scatters breadcrumbs that the birds peck up. 'The forest,' Mimi whispers solemnly, 'is filled with wolves and ogres who can sniff out a child's meat!' And then she pretends to nibble at Marie's little toes whilst they descend into giggles. It is a snuggly feeling.

Except Mimi is not family, but is paid in coin for her embraces. One day Nicolas simply decides to let Mimi go, so that Marie can be sent to a convent school. On receiving this devastating news, Marie curls up in a tight, shivering ball in her attic room, like a nut in a shell, waiting for the fierce adult voices to stop screaming downstairs: Mimi furious, her mouth filthy as a chamber pot. 'Is this my reward, after all I've done for you lot? How can my family afford to eat now, you selfish, maudlin, stuck-up cunt?' Mimi never comes back up the stairs to kiss Marie goodbye.

The convent is how girls are educated in this time, but also another lesson that Marie's true work – in this life – is to be a good girl. She must not miss her family, or Mimi, or their cat. She must not pine. Must not expect to have her hair stroked again, or her feet tickled. Instead, there is French, Latin and maths; there is sweeping up the cinders in a rough dress. There are hours on her knees in prayer in the freezing chapel, finding new ways to say sorry for being born rotten at the core. To an extent, Marie believes this story at her young age, and finds she enjoys a certain level of self-flagellation – cold showers, barely eating, accusing herself of vile sins, stripping her needs back to almost none at all until she feels clean and light. She has a talent, she discovers, for self-control. Even stern Sister Ruth sometimes says, 'You at least are a good girl, Marie,' which makes her happy. Soon she gains a reputation for being particularly quiet and obedient, though just occasionally she shocks the other girls with a flash of something wise or sharp, revealing the piercing intelligence that she patiently hides even from herself.

At night, the girls sometimes tell Mother Goose stories to each other. Marie is pretty sure it's not allowed, although that's never been made explicit, but the stories are too coarse and pagan and pleasurable to be godly. Some of the stories she recognizes as Mimi's, but the little girls pace them badly; miss out vital plot-beats. Still, Marie enjoys listening – enjoys the secret, sweet knowledge that she could do better – and afterwards in the dark tells them over and over to herself in her head, embellishing, wallowing in the grief and jewels and kisses, and then feeling grotesque, bloated with story, and pleading with that God who knows every small thought that flickers through her small head for absolution.

Soon – strangely soon – it is her thirteenth birthday, although birthdays are not celebrated in the convent. After prayer she is scuttling between buildings in the rain when a hand lands on her shoulder. It is her father, hassled, twitchy, his wig dripping, bulging in a manner that gives him the look of a toad. Silently, he presents her with a rose picked from the convent garden: a warm skin-white, slightly bruised to brown at the edges, and it is one of the most surreal moments of her life – the wet hiss, the thick scent, her father's face so out of context she has to flail around a moment for his name. Father. Mon père.

'I remembered,' he asserts. 'It's time. You need to come with me.'

But time for what? Marie-Catherine feels herself being caught up as if in a river, or history, or God's will, something pulling her forward. She tries to empty her mind as the coachman starts to grab her things – it seems they need to make a trip of some urgency.

'Does Maman know you're taking me?'

'We are of the same mind.'

'The sisters?'

'They'll learn soon enough.'

'Where are you taking me?'

'You'll see soon enough. A wonderful place.'

'For my birthday?' she asks, hopefully.

'For – for longer than that.'

Now in the carriage she still holds the rose carefully so as not to snag her dress and puts her nose in it, closing her eyes, trying to lose herself in the sweet scent; her father's one tiny kindness. But rain pummels the roof and the wet, potted roads get darker and rougher; trees twist like hands. The hoof-taps of the horses pound like her racing heart. They seem to tap out the message: *terrible, terrible, terrible.*

Evening falls. Her father, who has always had a weak, wheedling voice, hardly speaks on the hour's journey, as though he knows with this act that he is severing something between them. He is hunched with shame beside his crooked shadow, hiding his face in his hands by and by, like a man who has lost a great deal on a single bet. 'It's for the best,' he says finally as they pull up outside the gleaming building, his eyes horribly wet. 'The convent's no real life, you know that. And money is money, so. It's been a hard year even for the nobles, your mother's had to return some of her jewels. We must take our opportunities. Chin up, my flower.'

'But Sister Ruth, what will she think when I'm gone?' Marie asks. The thought of displeasing her fills Marie with horror. The thought of being the bad girl in the story.

'What does it matter?'

'She'll think I've forsaken my faith!'

'Don't be silly, child. God alone is our judge.'

As they arrive at the household of the Duke of Vendôme, he presses a final brusque kiss into her hair, and takes a sniff, as from a bud. Then he leads her up the thick marble steps, over the gilt threshold, through a long hall, and into a grand, busy room – one boiling with hundreds of candles, music, big drunken voices – to introduce her to her future husband.

The Baron d'Aulnoy recently purchased his title from his friend, the duke. He is comfortable in the duke's occasional absences, as a sort of second in command, keeping the party going. The first thing Marie sees when she looks up at him are teeth, long and yellow and coated with slaver, protruding from the grey-streaked beard. 'Ah, so you're to be my little wife,' the Baron d'Aulnoy says, putting his hand of cards down softly, voluptuously, on the table. 'Welcome!' He opens his arms as if offering everything, his own groin at the centre. He is very tall, thickly set, making big gestures like a baron in a play. Other features come into focus: hair fogged with rice powder, a thin nose, bird-foot laughter lines, little patches all over his skin to hide the divots of the pox.

'Dear Marie-Catherine. Mon poussin. A pleasure to meet you, you may call me François.' Grasping her hand, he scrapes it lightly with his wet teeth, as though tasting her skin. The giggling courtiers; the hundred thousand flames. Her small fingers in his paw.

And they live happily ever after.

Or so some might say, those whose interests – political and financial – are served by young women being married off, but who would rather not think about what happens next. Actually, it is hard for Marie herself to remember the next few years of her life, the facts of which she presses down so deeply inside herself that it is almost as if they never occur. It is only sometimes when she sees bright red berries against the snow, or a girl with lips like a bloodstain and skin as pale as a sheet, that a vertiginous feeling comes over her, as though she might drop over the edge of the world.

Years later, she will refuse to remember the baron's thick, leering penis. His moist mouth choking out, 'You're mine now,' into her hair as he rapes her. The feeling she has of being smashed inside; the splinters of broken glass rubbed into her tenderest parts.

Or her first period, that curse that she does not understand: sitting on the fine, gilded cream-upholstered chair, seeing the red seep from the corner of her skirt; shaken with shame and terror. The baron's shit-eating grin when he finally sees it; how he licks his lips and says, 'Yum, yum,' and his cousins laugh.

She will refuse to think of the red bed where she pleads for mercy, racked as if for treason; her baby, finally, mercifully, slopping out and squalling. Her little lamb. Or finding her baby dead in its bed, like a doll she is too old for. Ice to the touch; the grey of old snow. How she howls and beats her head against the wall as if to break it.

Rose red. Snow white. Rose red. Snow white.
Rose red,
   snow white,
      rose red,
         snow white,
rose red snow white rose red snow white
rose red snow white rose red snow white.

There are stories, though. She begins to see the world is numbed by stories; everyone stumbling around drunk on stories, disregarding the truth. Stories about how marriage is a contract with God; about how bleeding between your legs means you are a woman; about how a husband cannot rape a wife; about how marriage is a happy ending. The story that a baron is better than a servant. That a baby who dies has been called to their maker in Heaven. That good girls are rewarded. Stories through which people see the true shape of the world only dimly, as through stained-glass windows.

Well, she can tell stories too. Marie, you see, may not be loved but she is clever and brave, and will write her own story with herself as heroine, simply editing out all the bits she can't endure. During her long, empty days, whilst the baron drinks with his friends, she escapes into books, reading widely from the duke's libraries; educating herself. She begins to write letters to her parents every day about her wonderful new life as Dame d'Aulnoy – using them to try on a knowing, literary voice – but when they almost never reply, she fills the hours by writing her own stories instead. Mother Goose tales. The pen is a magic wand she can tap and a door somewhere else appears.

Here – this is a book she began shortly after her marriage – you will see very neatly inscribed on the first page:

Marie-Catherine Le Jumel de Barneville-La-Bertran, Dame d'Aulnoy, wrote this at the age of fourteen years and eight months. Whoever finds this book should know that it was mine. Adieu, reader – if you have opened this book and I don't know you, I wish you ringworm, scabies, fever, plague, measles and a broken neck. May God protect you from my curse.

Oh my, when she writes, what teeth she discovers she has! And underneath there is a short tale. She has called it 'The Good Girl':

When she heard her parents whisper, 'We can't just watch her starve,' the good girl filled her pockets with white stones. Later that day, they led her deep into the forest whilst she let the stones tumble from her pockets. Once abandoned in the tangled dark, the good girl waited a polite amount of time, then followed the stones back home. They formed a shining path to the house where there was no food and she was not wanted.

3. The Tale of Donkey-Skin, Part Two

'The princess, meanwhile,' Charles Perrault says, more quickly now, wanting it over, aware of a new dark energy tinkling around the room since he mentioned Donkey-Skin's escape, trying to judge if Madame d'Aulnoy is bristling or tearing up or scowling without looking at her, which is hard, but aware too that the Princesse de Conti has raised a blonde eyebrow expectantly as she takes a deep huff of her pipe. 'The princess travelled for days and nights until she was starving and her feet bled. Finally, she came to a farm in another kingdom where they needed some wretch to rinse the dishcloths and clean out the pigs.

'On Sundays, Donkey-Skin would be allowed an hour's rest so would go to her room and bathe. Then she would tap the wand, open the chest, and try on one of her impossible dresses in front of the mirror. Even though they reminded her of her father, she would sometimes feel a moment of happiness, or perhaps pride is the word, at seeing herself young again, and why not? She needed this stolen second. Now, as it happened a prince often stopped at this farm on his return from the hunt. One day, lost amongst the courtyards, he came to the door of Donkey-Skin's tiny room and, by sheer chance, he put his eye to the keyhole.'

A titter now, from the tall young man, like water gurgling from a decorative fountain. Madame Angélique Tiquet, a woman who collects pretty boys and perhaps counts this one amongst them, gives a fond smile then drains her chocolate. The room has relaxed again.

'It was a Sunday,' Perrault continues, letting a twinkle into his voice. 'And Donkey-Skin was putting on her dress of jewels which shone as brightly as the sun. The prince felt faint at her beauty. Three times he raised his hand to knock on her door, but something stopped him.'

'Was it shame, I wonder?' Henriette audibly whispers to the Princesse de Conti, whose eyes laugh back.

'That night, returning to his father's palace, the prince was withdrawn and ate nothing. By the next day he had sunk into a deadly melancholy. When asked why, he spoke wildly of a beautiful maiden that lived in squalor, but they could only think he meant Donkey-Skin, who was quite the vilest creature one could find, and – they sneered – could hardly be the cause of love when she was a certain cure for it. Still, when his mother, the queen, asked him what she could do to help, the prince garbled something incoherent about Donkey-Skin making him a cake.

'"Heaven forbid," a courtier said, "Donkey-Skin's a drab, grubby servant."

'"It makes no difference," replied the queen, stony-faced. "Do whatever he says."

'So it was that Donkey-Skin took some flour, which she had ground especially fine, sugar, butter and fresh eggs and shut herself alone in her room to make the cake. She washed her face and hands and put on her moon-coloured dress in honour of the task. Now, the story goes that, working perhaps a little too hastily, Donkey-Skin's ring fell into the batter. Some, aware of how the story ends, have suggested that she dropped the ring on purpose, but who really knows?

'Whatever her intentions, the prince found the cake so delicious that in his hunger, he almost swallowed the ring. But then he saw that band of gold the shape of Donkey-Skin's finger, and stowed the ring under his pillow. Still his illness worsened every day, until finally the doctors, unable to cure him, sombrely concluded that he was sick with love. Now, marriage, whatever you say against it, is an excellent remedy for love sickness . . .'

Perrault gets a big laugh for this. He feels relieved, yes, he has definitely ridden the awkwardness out, and he knows how the salons love such cynical, easy jokes, although he doesn't mean it. He loved his own wife deeply. Every day he would wake and see her head beside him on the pillow, warm and crumpled, and feel a little rush of delight, that she existed, and was his. And now he wakes and remembers she is gone each day afresh – a small grey shock, a spoonful of bitterness – and he cannot think of her head on the pillow except it is strained and shining with fear, and he is Orpheus watching her face slide screaming away from him into the endless dark – no, no, he will not. He will not think it.

It wounds him suddenly, that this light-hearted gathering might assume he is cynical about marriage or fell out of love with his wife. Has he committed some small betrayal, again? Every day he is alive without her, absent-mindedly enjoying a piece of cheese or humming a tune, every joke he makes, it feels like some small betrayal. *Is* some small betrayal. And perhaps it has been his undoing, this grief – he has lost the ebullience, the optimism, which he knows made up much of his appeal at Versailles, where everyone must believe everything is the best, and for the best.

Where was he? 'And so, it was decided that the prince was to marry,' Perrault continues, realizing his timing is off now, he has lost wit's momentum in his moment of despondency. Still, on he goes – this is the beauty of the old tales known by heart, how the narrative trots from his tongue almost thoughtlessly: '"But I insist," the prince said, "that I will only wed the person this ring fits." This unusual demand surprised the king and queen, but who dares object when their beloved is fading away?

'The search began for the woman who could fit the ring on her finger. Gossip throughout the land insisted that to win the prince, you had to have a very slender finger. Charlatans were soon selling secret, patented methods to make fingers slim – trimming off a small piece; peeling it like a turnip; scalding off the skin with a certain liquid.

'At last, the trials began with the princesses, marquesses and duchesses, but their fingers – although naturally delicate – were too big. Next came countesses, baronesses and all the other miscellaneous nobility. Then the working girls. With grim necessity, they turned to servants, kitchen help, slaves and, finally, poultry keepers, with their red, soiled hands. Putting the tiny ring on their thick fingers was like trying to thread a rope through the eye of a needle. All was in vain. At last, the trials were finished except for Donkey-Skin, in her far corner of the farm kitchen. But who could dream that she would be a queen?

'"Why not?" bleated the prince with the last of his strength. "Please ask Donkey-Skin to come here." At that, some started to laugh; others objected to bringing that frightful, stinky creature into such a splendid room. But when she drew out from under the donkey-skin a little hand as pale as bone china and the ring slipped on to her finger perfectly, everyone was astounded. The prince and princess shared the kiss of true love.

'They prepared to take her to the king at once, but she asked that she be permitted to change her clothes. To tell the truth, there was some amusement at this request, but when she arrived at the palace in her beautiful dress the colour of summer skies, with her eyes the same blue and her waist so slender that two hands could have encircled it, then even the ladies of the court, by comparison, lost their charm. The king did not fail to notice his prospective daughter-in-law, whilst the queen was overjoyed. The prince himself found his happiness almost more than he could tolerate.

'Preparations for the wedding were begun at once, and the kings of all the surrounding countries were invited, even from the east, fearsome-looking on their ponderous elephants. And then, there he was – the bride's father. He recognized his daughter and begged her forgiveness. "How merciful God is," he said, "to let me see you again." Weeping with joy, he embraced her tenderly. His happiness was shared by all, and the future husband was delighted to discover that his father-in-law was such a powerful king.'

At this, Henriette de Murat lets out a snigger, breaking the story's spell. 'Delighted! I'm sorry but I bet he was delighted! Monsieur, your prince is an absolute bastard. A spineless creep. I mean, all the cake and ring business was completely unnecessary; all he had to do was knock on her door! How did he make it so complicated? And now he's excited about his perverted father-in-law being well connected? Is the moral of your story that men are abject arseholes?' She always talks dangerously quickly, as if carried by the momentum of her thoughts, not knowing on to what shore they will cast her.

'Not quite,' Perrault chuckles, good-humouredly.

'Please mind your French, Madame de Murat!' the abbé tuts. He is a scholar of all the deceased languages – Latin, Greek, Hebrew and Syriac – and it often seems that any phrase spoken by a warm and breathing lady's mouth offends his delicate sensibilities. He is also a connoisseur of euphemism – a man who refers to sexual intercourse, with a stiff, faraway smirk, as 'crunching upon an apple' and to prostitutes as 'nymphs of the pavement' – and so always finds Henriette's directness distasteful. Unable to hold her steely gaze, his eyes avert downwards, accidentally brushing over her décolletage.

'And the king embraced her "tenderly"? What an adjective,' Henriette continues, disgust seeping into her voice as that hypocritical abbé stares at her tits. 'You don't mention how she felt about that. Was she rigid with terror, I wonder, wanting to throw up? Where are the tales in which kings are punished for their misdeeds?'

'All's well, at least.' Perrault tries to smile, keeping it light whilst attempting to reassert his authority over the tale; speaking as to a daughter. 'Her father disrupted the natural order, but now everything has returned to its rightful place, as God intended' (he says this glancing at the abbé, instinctively sensing the man must be continually mollified, but he is otherwise distracted). 'I like to think that the moral of this tale is that it is better to undergo the greatest hardships rather than to fail in one's duty.'

'One's duty to what,' Madame d'Aulnoy's clear voice asks from by the fireplace, 'if not the king?' Charles Perrault turns to his hostess. Her head is tilted back slightly, and he can detect the tremor of adrenalin in her straight-backed posture. Charles is used to the paranoid atmosphere of Versailles, but even here, to speak so plainly of royalty is surely a risk.

'To goodness,' Perrault replies, carefully. 'Of which our own king, God save him, is the embodiment, though others perhaps less so. But still, we must respect that God has put them there for a reason. Such is, as I'm sure you have heard in the abbé's sermons, the doctrine of divine right.'

'But who decides what is good? Which man decides that?'

'A fair point. Shall we agree the moral, then, is not to judge by appearances? You will concede that at least?'

'But it is her slender fingers that reveal her noble character, is it not, Monsieur Perrault? Your servants are fat-fingered. Your moral is not so clear-cut.'

'I must admit, I did not realize this salon of fairy tales was also such an arena of criticism, madame. Perhaps I took a wrong turn and accidentally told the old wives' tale of "Donkey-Skin" to the Académie Française.'

Some laugh. Madame d'Aulnoy does not.

'You're right, though,' he acknowledges, folding gracefully under her gaze. 'Perhaps I need to work on my moral. But I like to end it so: the story of "Donkey-Skin" may be hard to believe, but so long as there are children, mothers and grandmothers in this world, it will be remembered.'

'Oh, it is really not so hard for a woman to believe,' Henriette remarks, darkly. 'There are Donkey-Skins on every street of Paris if you but look, sire.'

'We are not here for reality, though,' Perrault states, mustering his authority. 'Surely? That is not why we come to this' – he gestures around at the room – 'this bright-spot of civilization, this Parnassus! We come to escape into the human imagination, which spins gold from the straw of base reality! This is art's great pleasure. Madame d'Aulnoy, if you'll permit me, your story earlier – the blue bird visiting his beloved in her captivity each night with jewels in his beak; the wonderful mirror where each appear as they wish to be; the egg that holds a golden carriage; the talking pie! It filled me with wonder, and with nostalgia, a Greek word that means, as I'm sure you know, "the pain from an old wound". An ache! A true conte de fées – to use your own term, madame – gives us back that vivid radiance of childhood. It returns us to a self that we thought lost.'

Charles is laying it on a bit thickly, perhaps, as he knows his own story touched on real things – powerful nobles; the world's brutal inequities; the foul desires of men. But he also knows that these salons are only spared the scrutiny of literary censors because they are said to trade in fripperies. What did that critic, de Villiers, say again? That these 'lazy and trivial' women amuse themselves with frivolous stories 'in the same way they play with a fly or a ribbon'. Perrault had thought to come here for amusement, to distract him from his home's painful absences. He had thought to come here to escape politics.

'Perhaps we are too hard,' Madame d'Aulnoy says, at last, deciding to settle it. She can't quite find it in herself to snub Perrault after such eloquent words in praise of her salon. Also, she can see now how keenly he wants to be liked, which makes her warm to him a little. 'It's just your reputation precedes you, Monsieur Perrault. It was a very fine tale, for your first time – witty, beautiful, not a word wasted. Bravo.'

There is applause then at this cue, a polite, bright scattering, his cousin Télésille clapping hardest. Music strikes up. To encourage circulation, there are a few small beechwood and ebony tables, carved and partially gilded, upon which macaroons are laid in tall, pastel piles or trays of raspberry and gooseberry cordials materialize.

'Why, Charles Perrault!' the abbé exclaims, tottering unavoidably towards him – man towards man – in his high heels. His wig is the colour of church candles, whilst his eyes always perch atop enormous pouchy eye-bags, as if his face wishes you to know that he stays up all night versifying. 'I have not seen you at my court sermons since your wife crossed over to join her master in Heaven, praise be. You're just the fellow, though – I'm very keen to be welcomed, as it were, into the Académie Française, whose hallowed halls you mentioned just before – it seems the natural step for a man of letters such as myself, who has given over so much of my life in service of the literary world – and I was imagining that you could advise me as to how one is to secure an election when a seat becomes vacant.' The abbé sees salons primarily as networking opportunities, and has never been afraid to promote his own genius – his last book, *Gallant Verse*, interspersed the poems with adulatory letters about them from his admirers.

'It is a lifetime post, though, and I hope none of us will meet our maker any time soon,' Perrault tells him, firmly.

'Naturally, but God works in mysterious ways, does he not? One can humbly hope! Well, I'm also looking for a publisher for my major new poem, *The Sacred Pastoral*, and I believe you know Barbin, who has his shop near Sainte-Chapelle . . .' Yes, of course, Charles thinks. Rhyming couplets pour from the abbé unrelentingly, like shit down the new Paris sewers, always seeking an outlet.

After a few minutes of politic mingling, all the while conscious of Madame d'Aulnoy's position in the room, Charles shakes the abbé off. He moves towards the drinks and manages to catch his hostess's attention, which he dimly realizes that he desires. 'Madame d'Aulnoy, I haven't introduced myself properly.'

'Oh, you need no introduction surely, all of France knows Charles Perrault.'

'Please call me Charles.'

'And you may call me Marie, if you wish, though I sometimes suspect every other person in Paris is called Charles or Marie. It distinguishes nothing but the sex.'

'It's true, I must admit my wife was also called Marie,' he smiles.

This Marie is not cold, exactly; his earlier impression was incorrect, for she has a sweet-looking, soft face framed by perfectly curved eyebrows – full lips, a little chin – and there is an amused kindness in her gentle brown eyes. She wears a pale blue mantua; pearls glow around the hollow at the base of her throat, where she gives a tiny gulp. He guesses that she must be at least in her late thirties but still seems youthful, only a couple of frown lines showing through the powder. But at the same time, Charles senses at once that her life has been a great performance, in which she must never show – for even the slightest moment – a glimpse of that mewling, needy self that resides in all of us. He wonders if her performance is so impeccable that she has fooled even herself that she is invulnerable.

'Congratulations on your tale, monsieur,' she adds, with an ambiguity in her tone intended to imply that she is still making her mind up about him.

'Not at all. Just a tale from my childhood I remember fondly. The credit ought to go to my nurse. She was a wonderful storyteller.' Perrault hopes this modesty will play in his favour. Many women find it disarming.

'How unusual, to hear a man credit anyone but himself! And to credit a woman at that!' Marie replies. But is she being sardonic? He isn't quite sure. 'Oh, you made it so dazzling and modern, though.'

'Incest never dates, sadly,' he says. It feels witty, on his lips, then a moment later less so. He has an uneasy sense of the conversation curdling.

'It's good for us to hear a man's perspective, we know you are outnumbered here.'

'It is good for me to hear a woman's perspective too, we outnumber women in our home.'

'You have sons?'

'Two. Since my wife died, I have supervised their education myself.'

'They are lucky, to have such an interested father. And you have never remarried?'

'I have no shortage of heirs. And I have not yet met a woman as clever or beautiful as my wife.' His quick wit cannot resist the call-back, although the second he says it, it feels glib. Comparing himself to that monstrous king; his wife to that narcissist queen. 'Not that she made me promise anything,' he half-mutters, half-laughs – and then, as they both realize this could be read as a declaration of his availability, there is a second of excruciating awkwardness. Perrault needs a glass of wine, not all these sickly-sweet, lurid syrups they keep offering up. He knows he's more charming after a glass of wine. He wants to ask: *And you are still married to the baron, Madame d'Aulnoy? The one you tried to imprison?* But that would not be charming, so he doesn't ask.

4. The Tale of the Poisons

To understand Charles Perrault better, we should perhaps explain a little of the labyrinthian path that has led him to this salon.

He is born into a bourgeois family, for example, and at fifteen drops out of school, so he considers himself a self-made man – though like almost every self-made man, if you turn him upside down and shake him the coins and tokens of privilege come tumbling from his pockets: in his case, a costly law degree and a job as secretary to his brother, the tax receiver of Paris.

In his early years, his fondness for finding morals expresses itself through rebellion, as he dallies earnestly with Jansenism and opposition to the Crown, but fear and age make a pragmatist of him – his literary ambitions only take off, he discovers, after he writes rather banal and sentimental poems celebrating the marriage of Louis XIV and the birth of the Dauphin, and he learns his lesson. Then fate has it that his dear friend Jean-Baptiste Colbert sees some spark in him and decides that Charles is to be his protégé. Thanks to this great benevolence, in 1671 he – he, Charles Perrault! – is elected to the French Academy, and finds himself in charge of the royal buildings at Versailles.

Versailles! It's hard to explain how much power the

word has. It was once the site of a simple hunting lodge, but Louis has replaced it with a vast, seething royal residence unlike any other in the world. By 1682, the king has even made it the seat of government; the de facto capital of France. It is a city of the rich, a living fairy tale, Louis XIV's fever-dream – and all of it in the open, so any tourist can stroll in and gawp! Here, let us join the tourists in wandering around.

Everything rotates around Louis XIV, of course, the Sun King whose robes are as splendid as stars; whose getting-up and going-to-bed ceremonies structure the day; whose preference for orange trees means they are everywhere in Versailles, in silver pots, the smell of their blossom mingling with the scent of urine (there are no toilets, only chamber pots and corners) and nobles who bathe just once a year. There are bowls of petals everywhere too, to sweeten the air, and the furniture and all visitors are sprayed with perfume – it is often known as the 'Perfumed Court' though nothing quite disguises the uric fug in the crowded corridors.

Let us walk through one such braying traffic jam of sedan chairs, beneath the corbelling in stucco and gilt. The king feels safest with all his nobles here, under his constant observation, as if Versailles is some early prototype for the panopticon. They are constantly under his gaze – if not literally, then figuratively, for Louis spends much of his time posing for artists and his portrait is on every wall; his face, surrounded by the sun's rays, gilded upon each door you close softly for privacy; his head on every plinth. He struts and gallops across every ceiling.

(Reproductions of such images have been turned into engravings now, and distributed widely across the country along with the casts of the statues, such is the king's desire to be 'everywhere'.)

Those curiously tall women you see are walking on stilts called 'pins' to lift their silk shoes out of the mud, and from their height sometimes feel like goddesses gazing down on clouds from Olympus, so busy is the room with preened puffs of grey and silver hair. Cows and asses stumble around, providing fresh milk for the king's many children, pushing their large wet noses into embroidered velvet curtains; rubbing their haunches beneath Titians and Raphaels.

There is Syrian storyteller Hanna Diyab, introducing the court to the wonder-tale of Ali Baba in his baggy trousers, a dagger tucked in his belt and a jerboa under his arm. The queen herself half-listens, grey-toothed from too much garlic and chocolate, surrounded by her little friends and yappy dogs. It's rumoured that one of her daughters with the king was born completely black, and so they keep her in a convent near Melun.

Of course, you must get used to the constant hammering of building work; dust; scaffolds. That is Charles's doing. Versailles grows every day, as though its tools are under some magician's enchantment and cannot be stopped. The south wing is for the princes of blood (the king's illegitimate family), the north wing for the hundreds of nobles. More than one thousand five hundred servants lodge here too – each role often inherited and jealously guarded: the mole-catchers are the Liard family, for example, the Francines are in charge of fountains, several generations of the Bontemps have been valets de chambre, whilst the Mouthiers are cooks.

One hundred men having watched him get combed and dressed, the king's procession is now making its way beneath the chandeliers, through the hall of looking glasses: a wonder that required the establishment of a royal glassworks, and the poaching of the finest mirror-makers and their industrial secrets from the Venetians. It floods with light from the big windows, reflected back by the gilt-framed windows of the mirrors. Can you glimpse the man himself through the simpering crowd that call out to him with their requests; slip messages into his hands? He adores shoes, so is wearing a pair that add four inches to his meagre height – diamond-buckled; leather the cream colour of scallop-meat, with roe-coloured straps and heels. Ivory tights show off his muscular, dancer's thighs. A little belly hangs above them, a sign of wealth and fashion – some men at court have taken to padding their midriffs in mimicry. The royal robes are decorated with golden lilies and trimmed with ermine fur, and perched on top of the king's head is one of his vast collection of wigs: an enormous hive of dark curls chosen to make him look taller and virile. Lost amidst it all is that small, delicate-featured face – rosebud-lipped, shy with smallpox scars. A face you might take for that of a sweet little governess, were it not framed by such masculine pomp.

And we can see behind him, amongst the courtiers, the king's brother – Monsieur, as he's known – painted and powdered, his eyelashes gummed together; blinding with dazzle. His first wife was poisoned by a couple of his special boys. The king's son, the Grand Dauphin, is there too – tall, fair and broad, and obsessed with hunting. The Dauphin is generally viewed as a harmless lunk, though he has killed all the wolves in the Île-de-France – once six in one day – and before his own death will ensure they are extinct. The memoirist Saint-Simon famously notes that he is 'quite without vice, virtue, knowledge or understanding'.

After a trip to the royal chapel, in the afternoon the king will hunt in the forest, or go for a walk in the gardens. Come, let's go outside so we can show you the gardens! The king so loves a tulip that he imports four million bulbs a year from Dutch nurseries, whilst there are also abundant tuberoses, stocks, wallflowers, daffodils, jasmine, hundreds of fruit trees. There are thousands of fountains, ejaculating spumily with thousands of choreographed water jets. An orangery, with its universe upon universe of ripening suns.

What a view when you step out! The grand perspective. The gardener Le Nôtre's creation, every detail reviewed by the king himself. It is a God's-eye view: revealing a vast, intricate pattern of which those mortals below you, in the midst of it, are unaware. The symmetrical rectangular pools are positioned to reflect the sun's rays back on the palace. Then Latona's fountain, its golden frogs belching out water. The knotted paths and gardens; the box hedges; the parallel rows of statues down the sides of the great lawn, which unfurls like a green carpet, with sheltered groves on either side, and – far beyond, at the end of it – Apollo's fountain, in which the sun-god drives his chariot to light the sky. In the hazy distance the Grand Canal, where they have been known to stage sea battles; where the king and his friends go on gondolas that, with their costumed sailors who sing serenades, were a gift from Venice.

Come, let's go to the maze with its sixteen-foot-high box hedges, designed by Perrault himself, who advised Louis XIV to include thirty-nine fountains each representing one of Aesop's fables. Water jets spurt from the animals' mouths to give the charming impression of speech between the creatures, powered by waterwheels on the Seine. Within here are the Owl and Birds, the Eagle and Fox, the Peacock and Jackdaw, the Wolf and Heron, the Tortoise and Hare, the Council of Mice. The young Dauphin, you see, loved the fables, so it was conceived to educate and delight him – there is a bronze plaque with a caption and quatrain next to each fountain, from which the king's son learned to read. Now it is a fashionable place for romantic assignations, young people entering with their little guidebooks bound in red Moroccan leather, a fact that makes Charles warm with pride.

Whilst we're out here, too, twenty minutes' walk from the palace is the king's menagerie, with an iron balcony at its centre, the courtyards radiating out from it in sun-like spokes. The rhino is a suit of armour sprung to life; porcupines bristle with spindles. That cursed prince, the lion, licks his paws. The king is fond of animals, uninterested as they are in political gain, so makes sure that his pockets are always full of dog biscuits baked by the pastry chef. His dogs have their own cabinet des chiens, their veneered walnut beds lined with crimson velvet.

Every evening, after dinner, more pleasures; more wonders! Chandeliers flicker with a hundred thousand dripping candles in the Grand Appartement, where there is gambling – card games such as reversi or hocca, a sort of crooked roulette banned by the Pope, as well as aristocrats steadily sobbing in corners, stripped of jewels as if by highwaymen. There is a theatre hung with crystal lamps and tapestries that stages fabulous entertainments: plays with French and Italian actors; operas; the king's beloved ballet. One performance, *The Four Seasons*, involves some of his wild beasts: Summer riding in on an elephant; Autumn astride a camel; Winter hanging tensely off the back of his bear. If the king does not have too many letters prepared by his secretary to sign, he may join the audience, or even take part himself – just recently he played the god Neptune in a comedy-ballet. Other nights there are fancy-dress balls or masked balls.

Fireworks sometimes hurl themselves in the sky: a giant's white roses. Golden eggs breaking against a dark wall.

Finally, each night, the crowd gather at the king's antechamber to attend the dinner of the Royal Table. Another grand ritual: four soups – his favourite being crayfish in a silver bowl – sole in a small dish, fried eggs, a whole pheasant with redcurrant jelly, a whole partridge or duck (depending on the season) stuffed with truffles, salads, mutton, ham, pastry, fruit, compote, preserves, cakes. All stone-cold, for the kitchen is so far away that the king has never experienced a hot meal, and eaten largely with hands, for nor has he ever touched that new-fangled device the fork. For special occasions entire tiered gardens of desserts form pyramids on the table: precariously balanced exotic fruits, jellies and sweet pastes; sorbets scented with amber and musk; the wonders of the ancient world recreated in spun sugar and pâte morte; gingerbread palaces.

The king's appetite is legendary. At his autopsy, years later, they will find his bowels are twice the normal length. This is all the more remarkable given that years ago, whilst extracting his teeth, a part of his maxilla was accidentally removed, which makes him slow to chew and causes scraps of food to bubble out of his nose whilst eating, a fact about which he has decided to be scrupulously unembarrassed. These banquets have attained such importance within the court that when one chef, Vatel, sent the fish out late, it did not seem disproportionate that he then plunged a knife into his own heart in shame.

Poor Vatel, Perrault liked him: always focused on a piping bag, or tasting, stirring, darting around the kitchen with the energy of a grasshopper. Such a perfectionist about pastries! How he wishes he had told him: Vatel, it does not matter. Everything is just demolished after all by teeth and guts, then shat out into pots. Fuel for the royal maw. Even after such feasts, the king likes to finish by taking a handful of candied fruits, for the going-to-bed ceremony. It is his talent, his tragic flaw and his raison d'être that he always wants more.

And talking of bed and more, we must also mention the fucking. Did you see that maiden make eyes at you through her mask, adjusting the apples of her breasts? Did his crotch shove up against you in the corridor? They are all at it, constantly, gluey with fucking; dripping with fucking. Marriage is a political arrangement, quite separate from love, and not to enter into extramarital affairs a little gauche. This is a Paradise of Penises; a Cockaigne of Cunts. There are no common whores, of course – orders have been issued that if they are found within two leagues of Versailles, they will have their noses and ears cut off – but courtesans are quite another matter. The king has numerous mistresses, after all. Since he lost his virginity at fifteen to forty-year-old 'One-eyed Catherine', no girl has been safe, whether maid or noble. He takes his pleasure all over Versailles: beds, chaises longues, doorframes – a favourite is the Hall of Mirrors, unsurprisingly. He even has official and unofficial mistresses! The king's current official mistress is Madame de Montespan – or Athénaïs, as she likes to be known, and which we shall agree to given the pre-ponderance of madames – a woman of incredible power, and a diva both fabulous and frightening, depending who is asked.

You will not see Athénaïs today, though – she is receiving intimate friends in the marble baths. Whilst the king has only had three baths in his life for health reasons, Athénaïs loves to bask in water scented with vanilla, thus announcing her presence with a waft of haunting, smothering sweetness, like she pisses icing and shits custard.

Was there ever a place like this on earth? Is it not the apogee of human civilization, so intricately unnatural; pure artifice; that very castle in the clouds humans have always dreamt of? The perfect ending for every Mother Goose's story?

And here is Charles Perrault – we've found him – in the council rooms, arguing over architectural details, at the centre of all this: buttering men up, currying favours, shaking hands, making witticisms, charming the gardeners, sealing allegiances, always striving to establish himself, to seize what he knows is his moment, and prime, and good fortune.

But Fortune is turning her great wheel.

Charles first begins to feel that he has gone over the wheel's pinnacle and is in the descent when his wife dies in childbirth, but that is a private sinking, not registered by those at court, who perhaps don't even notice that his eyes are not so merry, his jokes not so quick-flowing as they were. Now, though, the drop is coming quicker, more visibly. There are rumours, you see, about Athénaïs, of whom Charles's protector, Colbert, is a close friend.

Charles finds it hard to question his friend Jean-Baptiste Colbert, controller of general finances, first minister, founder of the merchant navy – the intelligence behind the French East India Company that imports coffee, fur and sugar. Colbert who banned

Venetian glass and Flemish tapestry at Versailles, where they must now buy their own French products; who brought Bernini over; who gave pensions to Molière, Racine and Corneille. Le Grand Colbert. Raising his eyebrow at some new expensive scheme, and then making it happen anyway – going beyond, even, the dreams of the king, with as much efficiency and grace as allowed and always with an eye on the market. 'If this chateau must be the finest in the world,' he always tells Charles, 'let it be a shop window.'

Given that he is the son of a wool merchant, and has been quick to punish the privileged who pay less than their share with indirect taxes, there are some who see this financial nous as a marker of low class. Others caricature Colbert as dour, especially given his rumoured Scottish ancestry. But though his humour is dry and kept largely hidden, it is there. Colbert often takes a piece of bread to throw across the canal – if it gets to the other side Louis XIV will be in a good temper; if it falls in the water the day will be stormy. 'Not again,' he'll say with a wry smile.

Or 'How are you today, sir?' Charles often asks, and Colbert replies, with a shine in his eye, in his flat voice:

'Mustn't grumble.'

'And the golden goose?'

'Laying well.'

He and Colbert often joke about the golden goose. 'The art of taxation, my dear Charles, consists in so plucking the goose as to obtain the largest number of feathers with the least amount of hissing.'

But how has his wary, deadpan friend become entangled with Athénaïs? Where to begin? Her beauty is considered a glory of France: large, cool eyes; frost-blonde hair that falls in curls about her shoulders; a curvaceous, porcelain body with blue veins shimmering like ice-floes at the wrists. Some call her the true queen of France, but there are others, amongst whom Charles quietly counts himself, who consider her something altogether less benign – an evil queen. A wicked queen.

Colbert admires her esprit and her conversational skill, not to mention the fact she is a mockingbird, whose pitch-perfect impressions of all the irritating nobles Colbert has to deal with make him laugh loudly, and with a kind of relief. He also admires her sheer nerve – she is rumoured to have seduced Louis by dropping a towel when she spotted him spying on her as she showered, as if she were Bathsheba and he King David watching her bathe. At first, Louis kept her in a room connected to that of his other mistress, Louise de La Vallière, so that he could have access to either or both in an evening. But Athénaïs so outmanoeuvred her rival that Louise was soon sent to a convent. So successful have Athénaïs's machinations been since then that her illegitimate children by Louis have been legitimized and given the surname de Bourbon, a fact that seems to fill Colbert with gobsmacked admiration.

But being so brazen about adultery has brought a cost, some would say to the soul – priests have refused to give her absolution and let her take communion. Father Lécuyer is said to have raged: 'Is this the madame that scandalizes all France? Go abandon your shocking life and then come throw yourself at the feet of the ministers of Jesus Christ.' And it is dangerous to let such a creature feel unforgiven.

Suspicions around her began about the time of the king's affair with the Duchess of Fontanges – a pretty little innocent who tied her hair loosely with a ribbon, and was said to be 'stupid as a basket'. The child made the king feel young again; he presented her with a pearl-coloured carriage drawn by eight ponies, like a doting papa.

Later that month, two pet bears belonging to Athénaïs 'escaped' and managed to find and destroy the Duchess of Fontanges's apartment. Oops. Imagine the scene, the bears tearing through the apple-green damask with clumsy claws, biting the tapestry wall hangings – wrestling on the gilded four-poster bed; rearing upright to lift and smash the small marble tables with their vases of flowers; glass teardrops from the light-fittings snagging in their pelts! When this made both women the butt of jokes at court, Athénaïs's anger deepened.

It was then that darker stories began to circulate. The talk of poison began with the infamous case of Madame de Brinvilliers, who was tortured with that punishment known as the 'water cure' – forced to drink sixteen pints of water – then beheaded and her body burned at the stake, supposedly for murdering her father and brothers with what were known euphemistically as 'inheritance powders'. Following this it became the fashion to carry little pugs under your arm to the dinner table at Versailles, to feed titbits to in order to check the food was safe to eat. Reynie, the chief of the Paris police, was told to round up fortune tellers who sold such potions. But doesn't Athénaïs herself often visit one of these witches, known as La Voisin – a fearsome drunk who wears a velvet robe embroidered with eagles – provider of aphrodisiacs and abortions?

Whatever the truth, the Duchess of Fontanges died soon afterwards. Athénaïs poisoned her food, some say. Athénaïs poisoned her gloves. Athénaïs poisoned her milk. Athénaïs has been accused of trying to murder the king too with a poisoned petition, although surely that is going too far – his devotion must be far more valuable to her than his death.

Every day new rumours spread through the chateau like black spores. People are calling it the Affair of the Poisons. It is gossiped that last week she passed the king's other mistress, Madame de Maintenon, on the stairs, and Maintenon said, 'You are going down, madame? I am going up.'

Athénaïs expects Colbert's support. Does she also expect his silence? Perhaps he knows more than he lets on of her trips; her expenses. He has always kept such very thorough paperwork.

Then soon afterwards, Colbert begins to sicken.

Now Colbert has worked too hard, everyone knows that – rising early and working until very late. For a while his stomach has been tortured by the pain of ulcers, so he often only eats moist bread dipped in chicken broth. But Perrault can't help fearing something else as he watches his friend slipping from this life.

'Have you had the food checked, sire, for poison?' Perrault asks by his bedside, where he has brought Colbert papers to sign about the first French dictionary, his friend still determined to work even now.

'Please, Charles, don't be a fool.'

Charles grits his teeth, he whispers, with some effort. 'It is only – Athénaïs, Colbert, these rumours are putting great pressure on her; I fear if she is cornered, she is capable of almost anything to maintain her position with the king.'

'I said don't be a fool,' Colbert says, still stubborn. 'Don't listen to the bitching of these, these spiteful fops. She is the mother of the king's legitimized children. I helped her fight for that legitimacy. Why would she harm her ally?'

'Because you know too much,' Charles tries. 'Because you keep scrupulous records.'

'And I am also discreet, Charles. When have I ever been disloyal? She has the heart of our infallible and divine ruler. Do you think he is a dupe? Do you think us all so bad at judging character?'

The next time Perrault sees Colbert, he is a corpse.

In Versailles death makes a bloody scene. Having heard the dreadful news, Perrault rushes to Colbert's rooms only to find that Fagon, the doctor, has already declared his friend dead and turned the room into a butcher's shop. Lords and ladies stand by the bed as the body is hacked up into pieces, Colbert's head sawn open and examined, his wet brain like a clump of maggots; something grown in the pitch-dark. Liver and lights laid aside, his warm heart on a silver salver held by a duchess, his entrails a foul soup in a silver bowl. Colbert would sometimes joke: 'What a pointless farce. No doctor yet has said: cause of death my own incompetence.' But now it is no joke.

Charles thinks perhaps he will vomit. Fagon, in his black robe, is a peculiarly unpleasant man: ham-coloured, moist, hearty, his mouth always hanging open when he concentrates, with its lolling tongue. The doctor holds out a huge stone towards him – smooth as a pebble in his palm. 'In his urinary tract,' he says. 'I think this is our probable cause. Well done me. Must have pinched a bit. Ouch.'

'Surely poison?' Perrault asks.

'That is not a word the king wants spoken in Versailles right now, Perrault, you know that. Certainly not his lady-friends either. I'd keep that word to yourself! What did you say – poisson? No, no, it wasn't a fish killed him, Perrault. Wasn't some kind of malevolent cod! Wink wink.' He gets out his pen. 'This stone killed him, I'm writing that down. Urinary tract.'

It is the fashion in Versailles to grieve as noisily as possible. Afterwards, as they spill out on to the corridor, one of the duchesses starts to scream and moan like she's in labour. Others soon follow, all the panderers and flatterers miming sorrow as in a play, rubbing at their eyes, bawling and blubbing. Grandiose grief for the Grand Colbert. All of the spiteful fops he loathed with their hankies out, dabbing their eyes; on their knees; keening; falsifying. Wah fucking wah.

Charles feels a horrible noise rise from his own throat. This place. Can it be true that he has been building, all this time, with all his energy and talent, all his *self*, this eighth circle of Hell? Something Bishop Bossuet once said to him, when he first arrived at Versailles, now rings in his mind: that the city of the rich needs no enemy, for it carries the seeds of its own destruction. Oh, his friend Colbert, his true friend! Real tears salt his lip.

Behind him, then, he hears a pealing laugh; the click of high-heeled shoes. 'Fancy,' a woman's voice says, 'who would have thought they'd mourn their tax collector so?'

He smells the hot, heavy stink of vanilla.

5. The Tales of Anguillette and Red Riding Hood

The fashion for literary salons in Paris begins, it is often said, with the Marquise de Rambouillet, who claims to find the court of Louis XIII too rustic (and is also, frankly, an extremely idle woman who knows how to enjoy herself), so instigates the practice of receiving her closest circle at home in her most inner sanctum – her famous blue room, the chambre bleue, panelled with blue velvet and with a cloudless sky painted on its ceiling – where she lies on an opulent daybed nibbling sweetmeats, reading books and awaiting gossip.

Such social occasions, which blur the line between public and private, prove an opportunity to practise the sacred art of polite conversation. The gatherings are named variously, at first, for the places in which they occur – cabinet, ruelle, alcove – but soon the Italian term 'salon', meaning a reception room, becomes common. Enlightened noblewomen, unable to access formal education beyond convent school, swiftly realize that such spaces can also function almost as universities: as places to think and learn. 'Conferences' on philosophical or literary themes are instigated; poems and extracts of novels are read aloud; games of wit are played.

By the time of the reign of Louis XIV, innumerable salons have sprung up amongst the intellectuals of Paris.

This is partly a matter of fashion, but also, increasingly, of self-protection – Louis XIV, understanding that story-telling is political, has placed the literati under strict surveillance. One of the main jobs of the new chief of the Paris police, Gabriel de La Reynie, is to suppress any opposition or criticism of the king, so that anyone who circulates a pamphlet or flyer critical of the monarch is whipped, banished or sentenced to the galley, depending on Reynie's mood. He attends a lot of theatre and seems to particularly relish dramatic irony, for he is always seen to applaud loudest at the plays that are to close the next day. If you are perceived to satirize one of the king's mistresses you may expect all your actors to be exiled beyond the city's walls, whilst playwrights have found their work banned or themselves imprisoned on a whim. French writers do still have some freedoms – sex, vio-lence and coarse language are rarely censored, the primary sin during Louis XIV's reign being disloyalty. Despite this, though, the thought of Reynie poring over every metaphor or pun put into print makes publishing a newly fraught business.

Many authors, then, have landed on a more discreet method for writings and ideas to circulate: over private drinks in their private rooms. Not that this puts them beyond critique – women who attend such events, espe-cially, are often referred to as les précieuses, meaning the precious ones, which is either a tribute to their elegant manners or a slur, the playwright Molière's one-act satire, *Les Précieuses ridicules*, perhaps fixing the latter interpret-ation in the public consciousness.

The tale of Marie d'Aulnoy's salon begins at one of Madame de Lambert's equally renowned Tuesday literary luncheons. Everyone is still whispering about Marie's re-appearance in Paris – half-expecting her to be arrested, or her boorish husband Baron d'Aulnoy to turn up fresh out of debtors' prison and demand his conjugal rights – but how gracefully she enters the literary luncheon, despite this: upright and poised, pearls tight around her pale throat. Henriette de Murat, also there, is reminded of Odysseus lashed to the mast, so bravely does this mysterious woman endure the siren-song of gossip about herself.

The two women are seated together, happily, and they begin to converse: small talk about novels they have recently enjoyed. Then, after the soup and the fish course, the philosophical discussion of the day is posed to the diners. The author Antoine de la Motte sets the provocative question: is the ancient Greek poet Homer rather dull? This causes an intake of breath, and much laughter, before the debate begins in earnest.

'But I wonder whether we must not lay the blame with the translators?' Henriette asks, when it is her turn to offer an opinion. 'Surely it is they who have mislaid Homer's beauty and majesty. Everything they produce has the same effect, like they have eaten too much dust and are belching it back up in alexandrines.'

Her new husband, Count de Murat, bristles at this. 'You must excuse my wife,' he tells the gentlemen, smoothing their feelings. 'No man is safe from her tongue these days, even the scholars. It seems a wedding ring turns a wit into a scold.'

For a moment, Henriette is shocked into a rare silence. Her sharp wit having long been viewed as one of the chief attractions of Paris, these words from the man to whom she is pledged come like a blow. Truly, what does her husband mean? It is as if he were trying to humiliate her; to let her know that he is her master. It is as if she were some ordinary wife. Has she been deceived as to their relationship? Henriette experiences a grisly, rising panic. But then Marie comes so swiftly to her defence! 'Perhaps the question is rather why men marry and then lose all sense of humour,' Marie retorts, dabbing her mouth with a napkin as all eyes whip back towards her. 'It is hard for wives to find their lovers so suddenly dreary, as if some brandy-soaked old hack had mistranslated them.'

The two women's eyes meet then, a smile of kinship passing between them.

Shortly afterwards, when they arrange to meet in a chic new coffeeshop – where they sip black Arabian coffee, syrupy with sugar, from tiny cups beneath an engraving of the king – Marie shyly suggests that she cherishes the idea of forming her own little salon. Spending so much time with her young daughters, she often craves scintillating adult company, though cannot help but think that salons would be more enjoyable if the same dreary male poetasters did not always attend them. What could be lovelier than to discuss literature with lady-friends over cake and champagne? Her new home on the Rue Saint-Benoît has just the room. Henriette seizes on this idea, hungrily. They must invite the guests carefully – some of the women they most admire . . . Angélique Tiquet, an old friend of Marie's from her early marriage, will add some glamour. Henriette has met the Princesse de Conti, a great supporter of the arts who might deign to be a patron. They will invite the imposing, elderly bluestocking Philis, and Henriette's childhood friend Amarante (sadly, both will die within two years, of old age and measles respectively).

It is intended to be an all-female space at first. When Henriette jokes that it sounds quite the gathering of old wives, Marie replies that perhaps they should celebrate this fact by telling old wives' tales. Or Mother Goose tales, as they often call them: of ogres, enchantments and talking creatures. Since she was a small girl she has adored such stories. They could make a new game of it, taking it in turns to give them a modern spin.

'Aren't Mother Geese depicted as beak-nosed peasant women?' Henriette asks, unsure. 'Surely the company will be too fabulous.'

'On the contrary, to listen to such tales would make me feel a girl again, and all adulthood just a terrible dream,' Marie notes, her voice slightly wobbly with the truth of it – for, perhaps out of some kind of superstition, it is a long time since she has spoken her desires out loud in this manner.

'Well then,' Henriette responds – committing herself to this friend; this plan – 'I will acknowledge that such tall tales, being largely about marriage, are quite the perfect form in which to complain about husbands. Since becoming a newlywed, I must admit I am positively dying to pin epilogues upon their happy endings.' It is decided: they are going to have such fun.

Soon Angélique has asked if she can bring Charlotte-Rose, a close friend's god-daughter – it is a favour to the friend, who thinks the girl needs more female role models, for she is boy-mad but also bookish. ('Sadly, those things are far from mutually exclusive,' Henriette observes. 'Who would wish to kiss a man had they not read about it first?')

Next, Télésille – one of those demons of correspondence who exist at this time, who churn out two dozen intimate letters before breakfast – catches scent of this new salon, so begins to post gushing missives and drop visiting cards by Marie's home every other day, ingratiating herself until she too is invited into the circle.

For a year or so the group stays intimate and exclusively feminine. But then, after Marie coins the term 'contes de fées', or fairy tales, the fame of these 'Modern Fairies' begins to spread too fast – though it is flattering in a manner, of course. Saint-Évremond wishes to pay his respects, when he passes through the city. The abbé, newly published, corners Marie at Philis's funeral clutching a letter of introduction, and invites himself to read extracts of the volume to her gathering. It becomes hard to think of polite reasons quickly enough, to turn down Duchess this or Monsieur that.

There are sometimes two dozen attendees now, but despite the growing guest list, Madame d'Aulnoy still takes great joy in these evenings. She still imagines herself safe and amongst friends.

Now she has shut the door to the rest of the house – her three daughters, their housekeeper, the kitchen maid, Mimi, the greyhounds, the chiming clock, all the busy happy clatter of this story that she has written for herself – and she takes a deep breath. The candlesticks are lit, music is playing, and there is the low hum of gossip about Madame Henriette de Murat, as Henriette likely very much intended when she wore her red riding hood to church on Sunday, for one only wears a red riding hood to such occasions deliberately.

Marie begins to check that each of les précieuses has a drink, listening into little seams of chatter as she circulates: '. . . said the priest had angered her with two sermons in a row about the woman's role: is it the First Epistle to Timothy? "A woman must quietly receive instruction with entire submissiveness . . ."'; '. . . her father-in-law looked furious'; '. . . in the art of creating a mise en scène she is certainly . . .'

At last, the subject of discussion arrives, coolly, without acknowledging the time or the sudden, descending hush. Maybe we ought to look at Henriette a little more closely as she takes off her hood – her very white, powdered face, the skin still tingling with cold from outside, with a triangular chin; the black eyebrows and lashes that suggest ebony hair beneath the wig; her long amused eyes already seemingly scouring for provocation, though her bitter humour has a deliberate performativity about it, as if a child playing dare; a black velvet beauty patch shaped like a tiny moon by her carefully curled lip.

Henriette was born in Brittany. Rumours abound

about her past, apparently involving many affairs before her arrival in court, where she first scandalized Versailles by dressing in a Breton peasant costume – rumours Henriette de Murat lightly encourages, often quoting the maxim of La Rochefoucauld that 'Plenty of women have no affairs at all, but there is seldom a woman who has only one.' She has been taunting people for months with the prospect of a book called *Memoirs of the Countess of M****, a two-volume collection meant as a response to Saint-Évremond's forthcoming *Memoirs of the Life of Count D*** before his Retirement*, extracts from which seem to portray women as fickle and incapable of virtue. 'As if men were not the root of all evil!' she declares, indignantly. 'Although of course,' she always adds, conspiratorially, 'you understand I've had to lie about everything! I can assure you. No one wishes to read about my real marriage, least of all me.'

Now Henriette has arrived, the salon can begin properly, as it is her turn to start with a new tale – Madame d'Aulnoy always puts together a schedule, to ensure its smooth running. First, though, the hostess makes sure her friend has a glass of gooseberry cordial, for refreshment after her journey.

'Ah, marvellous,' Charles Perrault says, when they are told it is time to begin, for he genuinely loves the spoken word and believes he is about to get a very amusing show. This is only his second visit to the salon, so he has not heard Henriette perform before. 'I have heard great things about your accomplished stories, madame,' he adds. Her tale 'Perfect Love' apparently involved an ingenious underwater riff on Versailles – exquisite shell grottos mimicking the king's own Grotte de Thétys with its cunning hydraulics; a palace guarded by a hundred dolphins; ballets of naiades in gowns made of glittering fish-scale dresses . . .

'Not from other men, I hope?' Henriette replies, with her customary speed. 'My aim is only to discomfort the male of the species. You have tales enough of your own.'

'Here, here,' the Princesse de Conti says, a nice big glass of red wine by her hand, watching Henriette as if a graceful falcon about to land on her fist. Henriette flashes a little smile at the princess, who it seems is her preferred audience, then stands.

'This is the tale of "Anguillette",' Henriette de Murat begins, rehearsed and fluent. 'Now, to whatever greatness destiny may elevate those it favours, I think we will all agree there is no escape in this world from sorrow. Even fairies themselves have a burden to endure. Did you know that these creatures have the misfortune of being compelled to change their shape, a few days in every lunar month? It is true, they become their animal selves, whether that beast is celestial, terrestrial or aquatic! So it was that at her time of the month, the fairy Anguillette found that she transformed into a thick, slick muscular eel, whose skin glistened with a rainbow . . .'

Charles can see what Henriette meant about her intended crowd – the women in the room all look alight with recognition, whilst he feels an adverse twinge, as if being deliberately poked. Still, he appreciates her originality and her turn of phrase – a meadow 'enamelled' with flowers! Wonderful. It is a long tale – she is never short of words, that seem to pour from her in a torrent, but there is much to delight. The tale, too, includes a generous nod to Madame d'Aulnoy herself ('a modern fairy, wiser and more accomplished than those of years gone by') and, unusually, ends in tragedy – the fairy, rescued from being the king's fish dinner, grants a girl intelligence, loveliness and riches but she is not satisfied, wanting a life of passion. After the two rival princes she loves have a fatal duel, she flings herself on the point of a sword, burying it deep into her breast.

'Poor Anguillette could not bring the foolish mortals back,' Henriette de Murat concludes. 'But only touch their corpses with her wand, and transform them into beautiful trees, which we call elms.'

Applause begins. Henriette takes a small curtsey, then goes to perch on the arm of the Princesse de Conti's chair, the princess patting her back, gently, in praise.

'It's just too, too sad,' Télésille bursts out, dabbing her eyes, having taken the tale a little more seriously than its author.

'True, I can't believe you let them all perish, Henriette!' Charlotte-Rose Caumont de La Force declares, touching her lace gloves to her pretty lips as if to shush herself. 'Oh, my goodness, you're absolutely wicked!' she adds, with an embarrassed smile. Will that do? She feels she ought to comment, for she is aware that she never comments and people must be wondering what she is even doing in such esteemed company. But what drivel she comes out with! How little she contributes to the debate! Everyone must think her a perfect fool. All these writers, who have published actual books – her heroines – looking at her, and she just a lady-in-waiting (thankfully her ringlets look good tonight, at least).

'I agree, Charlotte-Rose,' Angélique says, for she remembers, occasionally, that she has promised to encourage the girl. 'Gorgeous ringlets, by the way.'

'But no one ate the eel!' Henriette tells Charlotte. 'Be thankful for my small mercies.'

'Not one for the children, perhaps,' Charles says with a teasing smile.

'No indeed, I should hope not,' Henriette replies. 'For there are no children in this room to my knowledge, monsieur, although' – she nods towards the tall young man, Charles Briou, who has sat himself again beside the much older Angélique – 'it is true Monsieur Briou might be said to crave a mother's care.'

'Henriette, please!' Angélique squeals, trying to be game, although Henriette can be a little hard sometimes – everyone knows a woman's age is not an appropriate subject for jest. 'I do not have a maternal bone in me, as you well know!'

'You have boys, though, Monsieur Perrault,' Henriette says, looking brightly at Charles, as if spoiling for a battle of words. 'I dare say they play with their toy soldiers, repeatedly killing their dolls in complex and gory combat, yet I am not to kill any of mine?'

'They learn that men must fight for their nation and faith. And your moral?' he asks. 'Is it not to fall in love?'

'Not to fall in love with men at least,' she retorts.

Perrault laughs. 'Well, there is some sense in that, I'll accept. My next tale has a similar moral.'

Did I mention that Henriette's husband, Count de Murat, hits her? The thickness of her powder is not just a look, but a mask for bruises. Beneath her gown, across her ribs, there is a mottled stain, the tender pale-green rainbow shade of eel's belly. The count hates her sharp tongue more and more these days, but it appears that she cannot refrain from goading him with it.

Henriette has established her own methods of revenge, though – or not revenge exactly, for he suspects nothing, but ways of satisfying her own sense of justice. This evening, for example, the Princesse de Conti has offered to take her back home in her carriage – the Princesse de Conti who, like her, is a lover of women. The first time they undertook such a journey she sat rigid with panic, swallowing the rattling dark as the princess's smoky fingers touched her where she was dry and tight with fear – because she did not know how to make herself vulnerable; how to allow something to happen to her, to let go, to not talk at a hundred miles an hour. The princess was so patient, using fingers and tongue to slide inside her, navigating by breath; drawing out wet and salt and pearl, until huge white-capped waves knocked the breath from her lungs – hooked – gasping—

Twice since they have enjoyed such assignations.

Unpleasantly, though, as Henriette recalls this – amongst these beautiful, accomplished friends in the brightly lit room – desire seems to have soured into self-hatred, and the cool slime between her legs turns her own stomach. A darker wave crashes through her; with its undertow of nausea. For if God has seen these perversions – as He surely must have done, through her own eyes and the princess's eyes, recording as He does their slightest tremble or moan in his Book of Judgement – she is damned.

From a modern perspective, of course, it is simple to assume that there is hardly anyone on earth who has not entertained desire for their own sex, at least in their most private moments – human sexuality being as wildly beautiful and various as it is – and that she should simply love who she loves. But organized religion was and is a system of brainwashing, whose intention is to impose, upon intolerable randomness, a game with strict rules and loaded die whose winners are decided in advance. To declare oneself an atheist at this time required a level of intellectual bravery almost unimaginable – it was to step entirely out of the reality within which everyone you knew existed and into a new one, barely charted.

I am filth, she thinks, with the kind of savage energy that would have her slit her wrists that moment, were a blade close by. *The devil is in me.* Also, perhaps, she knows it easier to hear such harsh words from her own inner voice than from the count, who might make allowances – given his own dalliances – for an affair with a man, but who would surely actually kill her if he ever found out about this, having what he considers a great sense of honour.

She must find some excuse for making her own way back from the salon, though the Princesse de Conti will be hurt and frustrated, she knows, by such excuses – her big warm hand is still, now, on the small of her back. Why is she so wicked? Is her husband right, to call her bad? Though he is bad too. Their home a miniature Hell in which they devise cruel ways to torment each other.

'I'd be fascinated to know more about your decision to turn them into elms,' Perrault is saying, slightly carried away by possibilities of adult conversation after a fallow week. 'Where did you get that idea? I thought of Daphne pursued by Apollo, turned into a laurel tree. Or there's Myrrha, isn't there, who tricks her father into sexual intercourse and then he chases her across Arabia with his sword when he finds out – the myrrh tree's resin supposedly her bitter tears. The elm, though – am I right in thinking Achilles grasps one in an attempt to save himself from drowning?'

'Of course, no suicide becomes an elm, madame,' notes the abbé, as if sad to be breaking difficult news, his eyes dipping sombrely once again to Henriette's bosoms. 'Your heroine, truth be known, would spend all of eternity burning in Hell under the gaze of Satan.'

Perhaps she doesn't respond to this. She doesn't remember responding.

'Henriette?' Madame d'Aulnoy is saying to her now. Lovely, brilliant Marie, whom she adores like an elder sister. 'You seem distracted, suddenly. Are you feeling all right? Henriette?'

'Yes,' she replies, weakly, trying to swim up out of the grimy waters of disgust.

'I liked your tragic ending myself,' Marie d'Aulnoy

says. 'As Aristotle has argued, such stories are cathartic, are they not? You are the best of us, I think – our tales are warmed-over old soup by comparison.'

'No,' Madame de Murat says, sharp with sadness. 'No, Marie, you mustn't say that.'

'Here,' Marie tells her, offering Henriette a little almond cake, with a bonnet of rose-petal cream. 'You must try these – our cook's secret recipe. Rumour has it that anyone who tastes one will realize they are loved.' And she watches until she is satisfied that Henriette has taken a soft, fragrant bite, and that the magic is beginning its work.

'Is it my turn next?' Marie hears Perrault ask then, and it makes her feel rather irritated: his big male voice ringing out across her intimate coral room. She expects he means well, and is obviously excited – it seems he has spent much of the week zealously overpreparing at his home, out of habit and a terror of boredom, as if for a royal masque and not merely five minutes in the front room of a woman he barely knows, and has even got Madame Tiquet involved in the enactment – but there is something about a man turning up, after all these months, and commanding the space so unthinkingly that makes her inwardly furious. It also seems – as she gathers when Angélique approaches Henriette asking to borrow her coat – that he has chosen the story of little Red-Cap, which seems rather loaded this week of all weeks, and does not even have the benefit of novelty.

Perrault is beginning, though, after a throat-clearing,

a little glass-dinging: 'Once upon a time there lived, in a certain French village, a country girl. The prettiest little creature ever seen. She had a doting mother, and her grandmother – also excessively fond of her – made for her a little red riding hood. It suited the girl so well, soon everybody called her Little Red Riding Hood.' Madame Tiquet now models the hood, her face attempting to embody 'innocent girlishness', though like most of her expressions, to the viewer it appears more sexually loaded than the performer intends.

Everyone looks across at Henriette, who manages a pursed smile of tolerance.

'One day,' Perrault continues, 'her mother, having made some buns, said to her, "Go, my dear, and see how grandmama is – carry her a cake, and this little pat of butter . . ."'

Angélique marches on the spot at this, swinging her arms and whistling, and the tall boy, Briou – who is warming greatly to his role as the lone, dashing young man in this room of women – hollers approval.

And so on. I am sure you know this story: you know it from your mother, your grandmother, perhaps your nanny. Every beat – the grandmother's bed; the ears; the eyes; the teeth. For it is one of the stories that will be anthologized in Perrault's phenomenally successful *Contes de ma mère l'Oye* (*Stories of Mother Goose*), published in 1697. The covers or frontispieces of the many editions often show old Mother Goose herself, that archetypal storyteller – an ageing, sharp-featured peasant – sat by the fire with the cat or the spinning, children listening enraptured to her tales. But as it is Perrault's version of the tale such women have by heart, why replicate it here? Unless perhaps you think a woodcutter rescues her?

Madame Tiquet acts out being gobbled up very dramatically, much to everyone's delight – shrieking with agony before swooning away from probable blood-loss.

Then, at the end, comes this witty rhyming moral Perrault has clearly laboured over, which he reads in his best poetry voice:

> *Children, and most especially girls –*
> *pretty ones, sheltered from the world –*
> *should never talk to unknown men,*
> *who likely want to gobble them.*
> *For there are wolves with pelts of hair,*
> *whose huge teeth serve to say beware,*
> *but also wolves who seem quite sweet,*
> *when wooing women in the street*
> *with flattery and playful charm.*
> *It's very hard to see the harm*
> *till they devour you, blood and bone.*
> *Perhaps you keep one in your home?*
> *My moral is a warning too:*
> *that smooth-tongued wolf will ruin you.*

Naturally his Red Riding Hood, Angélique Tiquet, oblivious to morals, is curtseying before he's even finished his last couplet, lapping up her moment – the words just sluicing straight through her like a drink pissed away. Does Briou listen, though, Madame d'Aulnoy wonders, as he stands and embraces the actress of the hour, lingering a little too long – does he recognize himself in this description?

'Marvellous, Charles,' Angélique says at last after the compliments die down, glowing with plaudits, shrugging the red cloak off her plump, downy arms. 'Although I can't help but wish it had gone on longer!'

'Once again I admired your brevity, monsieur,' Madame d'Aulnoy says. 'It is a skill to so distil a tale and leave us wanting more.'

'Isn't it a truth, though,' Henriette de Murat notes, having revived enough that she cannot overlook such a verbal opportunity, 'that men always leave us wanting more, whilst we are expected to leave them fully satisfied?'

'I told the tale only as my maternal grandmother told it,' Perrault responds. 'Such a warm, lively woman. She would tell me to "lift the latch and walk in" when I did it as a child, and at the conclusion would eat me up, making me gibber and squeak with excitement.'

'But then you short-change us, Perrault,' Marie replies. 'One of the French Academy's immortals, writer of *Critique de l'Opéra* in which you argue for the artistic superiority of our current age, yet you bring us timeworn tales passed on from grannies and nurses? We aspire here to write in response to the great Basile's *The Tale of Tales* and Straparola's *The Pleasant Nights*, and do for France what they did for Italian folk tale. I would like to hear your own work better.'

This feels unkind to Charles, who inwardly cringes to see his faux-modesty served back up to him this way – he is not the only one, after all, who has inherited these narrative structures with their deep, old wisdom, and he laboured to make the voice contemporary and fresh. Surely she enjoyed the witty moral poem, which is his own stylistic innovation?

But Madame d'Aulnoy is smiling, not ungenerously. He reminds himself that such cut and thrust must be expected in a salon, and is not ill-meant. As a man, he himself doesn't need to worry about being taken for a peasant woman as they do.

'Touché!' he replies, gamely. 'Very well then, I accept your challenge!'

After Perrault has received further compliments, the group begin to disperse – these salonnières – some staying for a glass of wine first, others calling for their coachmen, embracing and expressing thanks, comparing the lengths of their journeys home, hurrying out into the frosty Rue Saint-Benoît, its modern lamps each haloed by mist. It has been another successful night.

But wait – stand here in the shadow of the stairs and you might catch the last two of the party on their way out, in the hallway, in a little dance of courtship. Having put her red cloak back on, Henriette is telling the Princesse de Conti that she no longer intends to travel back with her – she has agreed instead to take Perrault and Télésille's coach which waits outside – but the princess pins Henriette to the wall with a kiss, her tongue sliding into her mouth so softly and deliciously, like an elver. Henriette pushes her away lightly, painfully, with a shrill yelp of 'No, we mustn't' that sounds, to give the princess her due, more plea than a refusal.

Someone else watches, too, in the shadows: already greedily anticipating the telling of this story, for they know a person who will pay well to hear it.

Now tell me, dear reader, who is the wolf?

6. The Tale of Prince Charming

The next salon is a month later. In the afternoon before it begins, Angélique Tiquet is in bed with Charles Briou.

Outside is a hard winter.

I failed to tell you this earlier, or perhaps delayed this information on purpose – for how can you empathize with these dames and marquises, these privileged few, once outside with the poor in the cold, where we would surely have been, you and I? Conditions have begun to deteriorate. Louis has waged costly wars, taxes have become exorbitant, and there have been years of bad harvests due to the terrible weather. And then there is the cold. Even the aristocracy feel it, in their draughty mansions, some insulating their skin by smearing themselves in fat. In their cellars, wine freezes in its bottles.

And outside the mansions, rabbits freeze in their burrows. Apples stick in girls' throats. The snow falls so thickly there is scarcely air between the flakes; lakes are glass coffins. All of France has become an abandoned palace, glittering with chandeliers and crystal staircases, its gardens full of marble statues of sheep and cows.

The poor dine on their cats or the blood that dribbles from slaughterhouses. The poor dine on stone soup. Poor children are abandoned in woods and found dead in the morning, robins covering their bodies with leaves.

Or, when they simply die of hunger, stepmothers eat their lungs and livers, cooked with salt.

I am trying to tell you it is cold. I am trying to communicate suffering.

Do we then hate Angélique, her pink, pillowy limbs entwined with Briou's on the silk sheets beneath the four-poster's heavy curtains? Her fire is blazing; on the table, on a silver tray, there is a pot of tea and a plate of madeleines warm from the oven; her pampered white cat Madame Miaou, having been lavished with pigeon and cream, sleeps curled up on a cushion; there is every comfort. Why am I still fond of her?

It is quite the fashion, at this time, for the well-to-do to travel around Paris incognito to their assignations – the women often wearing a black velvet face mask known as a loup (meaning wolf, so-called because they frighten children) which they hold up by putting their teeth around a small button; the men covering the lower part of their face with an extravagant cloak. On this occasion it is Briou who has snuck over to Angélique's home in disguise.

Now his clean-shaven chin, uncovered, shines with cunt. Her breathing is still a little fast; her large breasts, with their very large pink nipples, splay above her cute pot-belly. They have just been re-enacting that version of 'Little Red Riding Hood' in which she observes, 'Grandmother, what a big prick you have!' and he eats her out.

'I should go,' he says, not getting out from beneath the thick blanket. It is hard to go out into the whirling snow, even with an extravagant cloak.

'Don't go,' Angélique says, squishing a madeleine into

her mouth in two bites. Her teeth are tender so she tries not to chew too much, but sex makes her hungry. Or no, sex always makes her feel nervous afterwards, as though once lust's spell is broken, her lover will see her true form, which is a flush little piglet. Since she was a little girl, and her mother would appease her with bonbons, she has always reached for sugar for comfort.

'I ought to,' he says.

'As soon as you leave the house all the poor people will follow you, black with hunger. My perfume froze on my dressing table this morning! Can you believe it? Will I see you at Marie d'Aulnoy's salon later at least?'

'Maybe. I have to call in on my father first. I was sent a portrait yesterday,' he adds, glancing over at her mirror in which they make an attractive pair: her thick lips smeared with kisses, mussed hair, his muscular arms. Apparently, Angélique's nickname was once 'the Masterpiece', although it was a couple of seasons ago now. When he looks at her close her lines are more obvious.

'Of who?' Angélique asks. 'Though I'm not sure I want to hear though, actually, if it's a potential wife, I'll be too jealous at the thought of it.'

'Afraid so, some Spanish financier's daughter. My father's been wooed by her father, it seems, and his enormous dowry. The artist is godawful at hands – or I have to hope he is, one of them is all big and squashed like a crêpe.'

'Apart from the hands, though, how is she? Do you think you could like her?'

'If the Spanish artist has painted her best side, I'd

say she's an absolute dog. Sallow, single eyebrow, a moustache – whiskers virtually! My father always tells me a wife is for business not pleasure, but my mother was at least half-decent looking. I can't help thinking the other men would sneer at me, to have to bed a little sourpuss-in-boots like that. Even if she churned out boy-child after boy-child, there should be a kind of shame in it – proof I'd dipped my cock in.'

'You're such a crude boy,' Angélique says, shaking her head. At this he lets out a clattering fart.

'Oh God, really?'

'You asked for it, I was holding that in,' he giggles. He has a high, giddy giggle.

'You have such a nice pert little derrière,' Angélique notes, sadly. She perceives that one of her beauty patches has come off on the pillow, licks it and sticks it back on her cheek.

'I am not so crude though really, you know. I should like to marry for love.'

'Oh, but then you'd have to be faithful. Wouldn't that be terribly dull? I don't like the sound of that at all.'

'Well, you haven't wasted much time being unfaithful. How is your second husband?'

'How would I know? Claude? He's been travelling almost the whole time since I married him. It gets so cold in this bed, I'm well within my rights to find ways of keeping warm! Although you mustn't say a word, of course, to anyone, because I think he would murder me in all likelihood – he has that proudness about him, you know. Anyway,' she adds, pushing further although she ought not to – perhaps hoping for him to say something roman-tic, to warm her later – 'what would you know about love? I thought I heard you say it was merely an invention of the poets.' The words have stuck in her head as rather cruel.

'Perhaps I shall be a poet,' Briou observes, easily dis-tracted by attractive images of his future self.

'You are more of a muse,' Angélique declares and then, clumsily trying to show her affection, doing a little boop on his cute button nose. He squirms, though, at this. Sometimes she treats him like a pet.

'Perhaps I'd like to be the wooer for once, not the wooed,' he says. 'You say I'm a fine figure of a man. Why shouldn't I win a real beauty for myself? A trophy for my arm. I feel sure I could win Charlotte-Rose, for example, who all the other lads were salivating over at the hunting party.'

'Charlotte-Rose?' Angélique asks, suddenly feeling stupid with envy. Not perfect, posy Rosy who she her-self introduced to the salon, and virtually took under her wing! A girl his own age though, of course, why wouldn't he want that? Angélique is terrible at hiding her emotions; she pouts visibly, like a small girl denied a sugarplum. 'Oh, but your father wouldn't allow that, she's not nearly well connected enough. And she's my friend's god-daughter, so I'd feel despicable shagging you behind her back—' She reaches for his cock, which is erect again already, thick, wagging like a tail; trying to reassure her like a firm handshake. 'I hope when you're married, you'll still want to visit me in the afternoons?' Her voice comes out a little wheedling.

'You are hard to resist.'

'That's kind,' she says, still sort of flattened. 'You're sweet.'

'Am I?' he says, shoving all his fingers into her thick, golden bush, how she likes it, making her gasp. Seeing her chance to keep him where he is for longer, she manoeuvres herself against them, starting to lose herself again in pleasure, bringing her to the edge of la petite mort. 'Beg,' he says.

'Pardon?'

'Beg.'

This is new. Angélique is naturally quite obedient – doing before thinking – so gives it a go. 'Please, please, oh God, I want your cock, please, please,' she says, and then, seeing how lust hardens his face into a sneer as she says this, more loudly, committing to the performance: 'Have mercy, please, I need your cock inside me.'

'You fucking crazy old bitch,' he says. 'You like it dirty, don't you? I'm going to tell him how wet you get. I'm going to tell your husband I spunked all over your tits and rubbed it into them, and took you up the arse, and felt my dick touch your shit. You nasty filthy whore. You want me to ruin you, don't you?'

'Please,' she whimpers.

'Say it! Beg!'

'Oh God, ruin me! Ruin me! RUIN ME!'

But though he plunges into her then, though she teeters on the edge, she fails to come. Perhaps it is because she catches the eye of Madame Miaou, who is now awake and licking her paws as if to suggest she is very unimpressed.

Meanwhile, twelve miles west of Paris in Versailles, Charlotte-Rose is imagining Briou in quite a different context. She is lady-in-waiting to the Dauphin's wife, Maria Anna Christina Victoria of Bavaria, known as La Grande Dauphine, who is currently having a dress fitting for the upcoming ball. The dressmaker is making small adjustments with pins in her mouth. 'Pink velvet trimmed with gold lace or azure trimmed with silver lace?' asks the Dauphine, who is regarded as a rather pathetic character at court – considered terribly ugly and possessor of a constant cough that makes the Dauphin himself visibly grind his teeth. 'Oh, how tiresome this all is, dress fittings do give me a headache. Trying to gauge what impression you will make on the shallowest of people, only interested in appearance.'

'The pink, it brings out your colour,' Charlotte-Rose says, feeling covetous, knowing how much finer she would look in it herself. What a waste of good dresses the Dauphine is! 'You should have the bodice laced up with pearls,' she adds, wisely, for she has a good eye. She should like to go to the ball herself, but her mother says they can't afford a new dress this month, and it is absolutely unacceptable to wear the same dress twice in a row – Louis XIV is very keen on nobles supporting the French luxury goods industry, even to the point of bankrupting themselves.

Charlotte-Rose likes fashion: muffs, velvet hats with flame-coloured feathers, taffeta brocaded with violets, jet buttons, capes, fans, veils, soft gloves, open-work bracelets set with opals, rustling watered-satin underskirts, puff sleeves, cuffs. She enjoys perusing the latest fashion plates, and reading which colours are 'in' this season in the newspaper, *Le Mercure galant*. But her things are never the latest. She expends a great deal of energy weaving her long, shiny, biddable hair into chic styles – plaits and twists, with bodkins and ribbons, or long ringlets called moustaches – because these require time, which she is rich in, rather than money. If she has a reputation for posing it is slightly unfair. With only a small dowry, her mother has instilled into her that beauty and youth are her only capital, so she is incredibly self-conscious about the impression she makes. She hates her nose from the side, and finds her small eyes, with their scanty eyebrows, look bigger when viewed from above. She hates a little mole on her chin and often cups her face there, or brings a hand to her lips, to cover it over. Sometimes she uses rouge, or carries a sweet lemon, setting her teeth in it to redden her lips. When she walks in the gardens, she sucks her stomach in, whilst twirling her parasol to draw attention to her slender fingers. But all this regard Charlotte-Rose pays to her appearance is not narcissism; it is simply anxious habit, and the elaborate rituals of her toilette have only one real aim in mind: to make someone fall in love with her.

Charlotte-Rose, you see, is a romantic. Her mother always loved wasting afternoons in bed reading romances and eating petits fours, and from a young age Charlotte-Rose would find these books lying around and pore over them – she particularly loves 'secret histories' of famous people linked to amorous intrigues. She loves the first, hesitant meetings; the lips touched to the glove; the yearning; the obstacles; the kiss. Oh, the kiss! The exquisite relief of it! She never thinks of what comes after, only that moment, in which a girl's whole life must tremble like the world reflected in a drop of dew.

She has practised on her hand. On the looking glass. And yesterday, she found herself imagining Briou, with his pretty, tender face. They are lost deep in the labyrinth at dusk, the nightingale singing, when they come across the statue of Love holding a ball of thread. 'Ah, a fine statue,' he says. 'It moves me deeply, for I feel I could find my way through this life if only—' He breaks off.

'What is it?'

'No, it is too painful, it cannot be!' Briou dabs a tear like a stray diamond from his long eyelashes.

'Perhaps you can have your heart's desire, sir,' she replies coyly.

'Impossible. I cannot hope that one as fair as you would ever stoop to . . .'

A fit of coughing cuts in on the daydream. The Dauphine gestures towards the table. 'Could you bring me my handkerchief, Charlotte-Rose? And have my letters arrived? I think there's one from Germany, if you could read them out to me.' She shivers. 'It's so cold in this palace, the draughts, the draughts. And Louis's insistence that we women wear French silks in winter! Does he not realize we're all blue with cold, or is it some kind of punishment? Make me a posset. And can this fire not be any larger? I really think this weather is terrible for my health.'

Charlotte-Rose is not yet fixed on Briou, you understand. There are numerous handsome young men at court she has imagined this way, but how can they fall in love with her if she is not at the ball, for them to ask her for a dance? She often feels like a violet hidden in the grass, that might be crushed before it is noticed.

At least Madame d'Aulnoy's salon allows her an opportunity with Briou – to converse with him. She might be able to perform before him, even, if she ever works up the nerve to bring the story she has been working on. And, as Briou sometimes joins in with the fancy dress, Charlotte-Rose has been unable to help noticing how comfortably he inhabits the role of Prince Charming. He is the most convenient young man for her to fixate on, and, as Madeleine de Scudéry writes in her novel *Clélie*, 'the river of inclination flows all too fast into the sea of danger.'

In her tale, a princess imprisoned in a silver tower in the middle of a forest has gorgeous long hair, and the lovesick prince climbs it. Isn't that such a romantic idea? Perhaps they will act it out. 'Charlotte-Rose, Charlotte-Rose,' Briou will say. 'Let down your hair.' And she will let down her hair, in a tumble! Although perhaps she needs to work on the character's name.

But anyway: 'Will you marry me, my darling?' he will say. 'Would you do me the honour of being my wife?' Or simply: 'Marry me.'

Marry me marry me marry me.

7. The Tale of the Little Glass Slipper

Evening comes with its lamplighters. Carriages begin to appear on the Rue Saint-Benoît from which noblemen and women – heaped-up with scarves, muffs, rabbit and beaver furs – alight on to the snowy steps outside Marie's home.

Marie watches them arriving through the fractal patterns of ice; the window-glass a blur of swans' feathers. She shivers. She is in a strange, heightened mood today, having ventured out herself earlier, to attend a service at Sainte-Chapelle, its brilliant stained-glass windows mottling everything red and blue as if with cold; icicles hanging from its gargoyles' jaws like fangs. How this chill makes her whole body ring like a bell! Afterwards she put her black velvet mask on and gave out food to the poor, their small rooms made into marble tombs by hoarfrost. Little children, with bellies full of boiled snow. A sparrow fell at her feet like a stone. How her heart ached to see beggars without gloves, fingers missing from their frostbitten hands! Marie ended up giving one woman her own, and had to sit on her hands in the carriage all the way back, as she listened to the horses huff and struggle. From the carriage's juddering window she saw graveyards where the earth must be too solid to dig; bodies stacked up like job-lots of angels.

All of Paris seems under a shroud. There is a terrible atmosphere out there on the streets: a sort of festering numbness; a catatonic stupor that could explode into violence. There are rumours of grain carts being attacked. Rumours of wolves stalking round corners, drawn in from the forests by hunger. No one has told the king, of course. His new mistress Madame de Maintenon tells people that he does not like to hear about the poor, for it discourages him. Sometimes a treasonous thought slips into Madame d'Aulnoy's mind: for if she is a camel who may not pass through the eye of the needle, then what is the Sun King, the richest, most indulged man on earth?

Still, though, she thinks. *I am here. It is now. What an absurdity of riches!* She feels it would be sinful to squander her luck. She must glean all possible happiness from this house, these lovely things, this joyful gathering of dear friends. Was Mary Magdalene not forgiven for pouring perfume on Christ's feet? 'Champagne,' she declares. 'Let's have champagne!'

After everyone has thawed beside the fire, they begin with a parlour game, at the abbé's insistence – he loves to play bouts-rimés, in which the salonnières shout out random rhyme-pairs, and he must make up a poem that joins them together. Whilst his unwavering Christian piety makes it rather hard for him, the abbé feels, to truly shine as a writer of fairy tales, he is undeniably the master of this amusement, requiring as it does a talent for spewing out meaningless doggerel. Within seconds of being given the rhymes (reason/season, ragout/

stew), he has made a big show of scribbling down a piece he entitles 'A Poetic Feast for a Lady-Friend in Need of Entertainment Following a Tertiary Fever', that he then declaims sonorously, his eyes bulging with expression:

> *A first course of solid reason.*
> *Epigrams are my ragout.*
> *Attic salt will give it season,*
> *Pathos makes a pungent stew . . .*

(I will spare you the rest.) Afterwards everyone claps politely – and Télésille declares it, on behalf of no one but herself, 'Bliss! So erudite!', adding: 'We are so fortunate that you bless us with your presence!' The abbé accepts this compliment with his usual humility, his eyes flicking humbly down to her décolletage, before he struts around for a while, in his little purple jacket with the golden trimmings, admitting that God has blessed him with a rare talent indeed.

After some mingling and nibbles, it is then Charles Perrault's turn to provide nourishment. He has been working hard on a more contemporary fairy tale, after Madame d'Aulnoy's previous remarks, hoping to win her respect. 'It is called "Cinderella, or the Little Glass Slipper",' he announces, cheerfully.

'Glass?' Madame d'Aulnoy asks, intrigued. 'But surely it is vair not verre.' (For the slipper in such stories is most commonly made of vair, or fur, though it sounds similar.)

'I have always thought the fur slipper rather a crude

84

metaphor,' Charles replies. 'Now glass, that's a modern material: delicate, pristine, dazzling.'

'Hard to dance in, though,' Madame de Murat notes.

'Only a true princess can dance so lightly on her feet.' The audience make warm noises. Charles smiles, excited, rubbing his hands together in anticipation. 'Now, Briou, you won't mind being my Prince Charming, I'm sure. But who would like to play my Cinderella?'

Briou stands up expectantly, grinning, to make his way to the fancy-dress box. He is not unaware that tonight he has been the subject of stolen gazes and fur-tive, fluttering looks, with a palpable tension vibrating in the air which is rather novel. During the bouts-rimés Charlotte-Rose definitely kept staring at him in a soppy mooncalf way, with her chin cupped in her palm, whilst Angélique was taut like a cat ready to hiss. It is quite glorious.

'ME—' Angélique and Charlotte-Rose say simultan-eously, sharply. There is an awkward moment as their two voices hang in the air.

'Erm, Charlotte-Rose perhaps?' Perrault says, trying to be politic. 'As you were my Red Riding Hood, Angélique.'

So begins Perrault's famous tale of 'Cinderella', a story that no one who hears it will ever forget. Even Marie, grudgingly, has to admit to herself as he performs that the tale is marvellous – perhaps the most beautiful told in her salon yet, and she includes her own. Like any great artist in the moment when they realize that another is their equal, she listens with a keen, flashing excitement; a rising sense that the race is on. Oh, his images! The girl cleaning up the dirty ashes in the grate. The glorious scene in which the fairy godmother turns a pumpkin into a golden coach; six live mice from a mousetrap into dappled grey carriage horses; a sleek rat into a coachman and lizards into footmen. The glass slipper itself, placed on a little cushion. Charles has a genius for images, that's what it is – symbols that glow in the mind, rich and radiant with meaning. And the whole thing rolls along so smoothly and pleasurably – Marie finds herself closing her eyes for a few seconds, and lets his voice take her to a far-off kingdom, and feels, for just that moment, as if she doesn't have to be responsible for everything that happens. As if she can trust in his voice.

When she is old and her long hair is grey, Charlotte-Rose will also look back on these few minutes as one of the bright points of her life. She feels born to play Cinders. Although she is no servant, of course, still she always identifies with the goose girl of fairy tale, whose special qualities are somehow overlooked. Is she not a lady-in-waiting, scuttling round after the Dauphine? Is she not herself denied the chance to go to the ball? She is deliciously aware what a touching picture she must make in her costume of pretty rags, barefoot, as she scrubs at the floor, and adores the scene where – at a tap of a wand (she goes behind a screen) – they become an opulent ball-dress and the audience oohs and aahs as she twirls.

When she dances with Briou. O! The expression on his face, as though he's deeply moved, tremulous almost. The courteous touch of his hand on her waist. How he falls to his knees after the bells have chimed for midnight, cradling her slipper, heartbroken. The electrical thrill of his hand stroking the underside of her foot as he slips it on – as it fits – that makes her shake with delight.

Marry me marry me marry me.

Perhaps you were not so dissimilar to her? We most of us begin our romantic careers by falling head over heels in love with love.

'Bravo! Bravo!' shout their audience, the applause fluttering over them like confetti.

Briou's memories of this evening will be different – what he will recollect later is a warm sense of growing power. And also Perrault's moral, which will stick word for word in his mind and come back to him often, like a motto to live by. 'Charm is the true gift of fairies. Without it one can achieve nothing; with it everything.'

8. The Tale of the Ram

How privileged we are to attend this salon! For this evening we also witness not just Perrault's 'Cinderella', but the first reading of another fairy tale, perhaps even more original, by Madame Marie d'Aulnoy herself. The fact of her own new story has been adding to her strange soap-bubble of delight. It rushed out of her pen this week, as the best tales do – how she loves that sense of being a medium, a vessel through which story pours itself. Although I use 'rushed' metaphorically, for in truth the ink had frozen and had to be periodically warmed with a candle as she wrote. Now she wonders if it is as good as Charles's, after all? But she wants him to hear it, to like it – to parry his thrust, and show herself his match.

'You have a new one?' Télésille asks, clasping her hands to her heart. 'Oh, what a treat, what a treat!' She is a true fan, and feels that being present for one of Madame d'Aulnoy's new stories must surely make her the envy of France. She is already positively skittish, thinking about the numerous letters in which she will mention – as a subtle aside – her presence on this literary occasion.

'I do indeed,' Madame d'Aulnoy says. 'This one is called "The Ram".' Télésille zealously shushes everyone and a hush falls.

The story she tells – I will attempt to repeat it as closely as I can, though I will precis a little – is in many ways an early version of 'The Beauty and the Beast', although the version you know, with the rose garden and enchanted servants, was written fifty years or so later by Gabrielle-Suzanne Barbot de Villeneuve.

'The Ram' is a tale of three princesses. The youngest, Merveilleuse, is their father's favourite, until one day she tells him of a dream in which, on her sisters' wedding day, he offers her a vase of water and asks her to wash. A man of violent temper, her father decides this dream is insulting and a bad omen, so orders her sent to the forest to be killed, with her tongue brought back to him as proof.

Of course, the guard cannot bring himself to kill her – what guard, in such stories, ever can? Merveilleuse has for companions a servant girl, an ape and a talking dog who all hurry to kill themselves in her place, in a rather grotesque and mawkish scene. After burying them, she is left alone, stumbling through thickets that scratch her skin, until she hears a sheep bleat. To Merveilleuse's surprise she comes across a large ram in a clearing, with gilt horns and a garland of flowers round his neck, reposing on a couch of orange blossom beneath a pavilion of golden cloth. But still, a ram, with his nose like an ink blot, flies on his white lashes, wool the colour of curds. Around him a hundred gaily decked sheep graze not on grass but coffee, sherbet, ices and sweetmeats, whilst partaking in games of basset and lansquenet.

Soon he takes her into a cavern, which is a gate to his

underworld kingdom. It has meadows of a thousand different flowers; a broad river of orange-flower water; fountains of Spanish wine and liqueurs. There are entire avenues of trees, stuffed with partridges better larded and dressed than you would get them at the finest Paris restaurants; quails, young rabbits and ortolans. In certain parts, where the atmosphere appears a little hazy, it rains bisque d'écrevisses, foie gras and ragout of sweetbreads. His palace is formed by tangled orange trees, jasmines, honeysuckle, and little musk-roses, whose interlaced branches form cabinets, halls and chambers, all hung with golden gauze and furnished with large mirrors and fine paintings.

The ram tells her the tale of how he became a ram. An old, ugly fairy called Ragotte fell in love with him, then led him into a trap whilst he was out hunting. 'You must love me!' she demanded once he was caught, pursing up her mouth to make it look agreeable and rolling her eyes. 'I'll be your little Ragotte! I'll give you twenty kingdoms, a hundred towers of gold, all you can wish for. Consider how low I stoop! I'm confessing my weakness to you, you! You who are less than an ant compared to a fairy like me. You must give me your heart. I demand your heart!'

When he explained it simply wasn't possible, for that is not how hearts work, she showed him her flock – made up of all the mortals who had offended her – and gave him an ironic smile, saying: 'You think you're a lion but you're just a sheep.' She cursed him to be a ram for five years.

'Since then,' the ram says, 'wandering in the forest, I have seen you, princess, sometimes passing with your sisters. But how could I approach you, being a ram? I'm so glad to have this chance to talk to you properly. I've been so lonely. Rule this place with me.'

The ram seems so passionately fond of Merveilleuse that she agrees to stay for a while at least. Every day he bounds and frisks up to her and lays down at her feet; nuzzles her hands. He's a fine conversationalist. She begins to be fond of him; at length to love him. 'A pretty sheep, very gentle and affectionate, is not unpleasant,' Madame d'Aulnoy notes. 'Particularly when you know he's a prince, and due to transform back fairly soon. The princess passed her days in peace, awaiting her happy ending.'

But the story of 'The Ram' does not have a happy ending.

One day Merveilleuse hears her sisters are getting married, and decides she must attend their weddings. At this request, the ram feels a pang he can't suppress – a secret presentiment of misfortune. But we can't avoid evil, and he hasn't the heart to refuse her. 'If you desire to leave me,' he says, 'I consent, though I can never make a greater sacrifice.'

She promises to return quickly. To aid her in this, the ram provides her with a chariot of mother-of-pearl, drawn by hippogriffins. She arrives at her father's court at the moment the marriages are being celebrated, wearing a gorgeous dress, and dazzles everybody with the blaze of her beauty. The king is so impressed by this strange guest that, afterwards, he leads her personally into a salon, offering her a vase of water to wash her beautiful hands.

'My dream has come true!' she cries. 'Look! I am your daughter!'

The king, who has long regretted his impulsive order of years before, weeps with joy to see she is alive. Her two sisters throw their arms around her neck and kiss her a thousand times. Merveilleuse cries and laughs at the same moment with joy. She tells them her tale.

But whilst she is engrossed by the king and her sisters, the ram sees the hour fixed for the return of the princess pass. 'She will never come back to me,' he bleats. 'My miserable sheep's face disgusts her!' As night approaches, he runs to the city. When he reaches the palace, he asks to see Merveilleuse, but the guards are now aware of her adventures, and don't wish her to return to the realm of the ram. They refuse to let him in. He utters awful sounds; bitter lamentations. At length, he flings himself on the ground and his heart breaks in his chest.

The king and Merveilleuse know nothing of this tragedy. The king and his long-lost daughter climb into a triumphal carriage – he will show her to all the cheering city, by the lights of thousands of torches illuminating the windows. But what a horrible spectacle awaits, by the palace gates – her dear ram dead on the pavement! She runs to him with a moan, knowing her unpunctuality has caused his death. She wants to die herself.

Télésille cannot help letting a little groan of her own slip from her throat at this.

'It was then admitted,' Madame d'Aulnoy says, completing her story in the held-breath of the listening room, her voice quivering with emotion, 'that persons of the highest rank are subject, like others, to Fortune's blows. How often we meet with greatest misery at the very moment we believe ourselves to have attained our heart's wishes.'

The reception is rapturous. There are cries of 'A marvel!'; 'A wonder!'; 'You have exceeded yourself!' Marie bows her head a little at this barrage of compliments. She takes a gulp of champagne to steady herself, lets its fizz seep into her blood.

'Your most wonderful yet,' Charles tells her.

'Oh, not at all. You are a hard act to follow!'

'Did not François de La Rochefoucauld say in his maxims,' he replies – quick-wittedly, he hopes – 'that "a refusal of praise is a desire to be praised twice"?'

'Ah,' she retorts. 'But I believe he also said: "We only praise heartily those who admire us."' Charles laughs aloud at this, admiring her admiring him.

'I suppose the ram wasn't terribly Christian, was he?' Télésille interrupts, trying to understand the ending. 'With those horns on his head like Satan, and that rather hedonistic underworld.'

'Indeed,' agrees the abbé approvingly. 'His death was a mercy.'

'I was sure he would become a handsome prince again and they would kiss,' Charlotte-Rose declares, unable to

93

resist looking at Briou as she says 'kiss'; his eyes snagging on hers. 'Oh, poor old ram. I think the story proves not all men are wolves, some are romantics!'

'Yes, some men are lambs,' Henriette de Murat replies. 'Best roasted with rosemary and garlic and served with gratin potatoes.'

'My darling Henriette,' the Princesse de Conti interjects, pointedly. 'Must you always be so very cruel?'

'Yes, I must,' Henriette answers, for her whole side is grey and tender, where her husband threw her down the stairs, and if this is flirtation she will have none of it. 'I suppose I feel it is my moral duty.'

Afterwards, when the music starts again, the guests mingling, reluctant to spill out – just yet – into the icy streets, Perrault heads towards Marie, keen to talk more about her tale. She looked so lovely, telling it – as though lit inside. She is lovely, he thinks. Though not for him, of course.

Still, it has stirred something in him – there were tears in his eyes at the end. He feels like an old, battered sheep some days, his heart breaking in his chest. All Versailles's gilt and orange blossom mean nothing when you cannot nuzzle a warm body. Never again. His head against her head. My God, her mouth: his wife's mouth.

'Marvellous,' he tells Madame d'Aulnoy. 'The end! Your moral. So very . . . I mean to say, my wife, God bless her soul, she died in childbirth. What was it you said? How often we meet with greatest misery at the very moment we believe ourselves to have attained our heart's wishes. Very true, madame. So very true. How I wish I had been satisfied with what I had already, and not risked her life so.'

'I'm so sorry,' she says.

'I should have left her alone,' he adds, his voice coming out hard and strange. 'I wish I had! What beasts men are. What nasty, tupping beasts.' There is a moment of silence. He has shown too much of himself in the moment; he feels slightly undone. As he takes another swig of champagne Madame d'Aulnoy feels a great wave of pity for him. 'Although I did not believe, quite,' he adds, trying to slip back into his worldly, indifferent critic's voice, though it now sounds horribly fake, 'that Merveilleuse would forget her promise. Women are more faithful in love, I think, than men.'

'Oh, I sadly disagree,' Madame d'Aulnoy tells him, and then, her voice dropping to an intimate whisper as a sudden urge to confess comes over her – to repay his confidence with her own – 'you know of my history, monsieur? Perhaps you have heard that a man once died for love of me. The awful thing is, as the years pass, I find I hardly think of him at all.'

And they stand there for a second, slightly shocked and somehow bound together, as though they have shown each other their bloody hands.

9. The Tale of the Isle of Quiet Pleasures

The salon does not tidy up itself. No magic broom sweeps up the cinders. The candlesticks do not bring their flaming hands to their lips to puff them out, nor do the champagne flutes dance down the staircase and into the sink. Marie has three daughters, a housemaid, a cook and Mimi the nurse, and now that the party is over they busy themselves.

If you are familiar with Marie d'Aulnoy's story 'The Elfin Prince', you will know that within it there is a fairy who lives on a secluded island only for females, guarded by Amazons, named 'The Isle of Quiet Pleasures'. These days, she thinks of her home as such an isle.

There are leftover eclairs filled with a chestnut crème pâtissière and iced with fondant, which Marie lets Judith, Thérèse and Françoise eat without plates, straight off the trays and into their mouths. Her youngest at nine years old, Françoise, always begins – rather disgustingly – by slowly licking the icing off the top. Françoise is short and dark with the most expressive face imaginable, like an imp's, though it's very lovely in repose, and there is usually a monkey on her shoulder – her pet marmoset, Belle-Belle, given to her by the Archbishop of Burgos.

'These taste like a dream!' Françoise says, already

prone to poetic exaggeration. 'Imagine if we wake up now and we're eating dirt!'

'Yes, dear Anne,' Marie tells her busy, silver-haired cook, who never seems to sit, and always has at least two pots bubbling on the stove in the steamy kitchen, 'you surpassed yourself again. I think perhaps you are a real-life angel.'

'Did you like the chestnut in it?' Anne asks, curious. 'I wasn't sure if orange would be better, although there wasn't much to choose from at the market at all today, and I got there at dawn.'

These days their nurse, Mimi, has a body like an arrangement of soft pillows. Salt-and-pepper hair on her head, plus one or two on her chin. She is still easy-going and tactile: a source of tickles, foot-rubs and the odd smack. She is finishing off the champagne left in the bottle: 'Mustn't waste,' she says. 'Cheers, my dear ones!' She takes a swig in toast. 'Well, I liked your story best, ma puce,' she tells Marie.

'You listened, Mimi?'

'I may have found myself in the hallway with an ear to the keyhole, mightn't I? Can't pretend I don't love a tale. You've never looked at a man and not imagined him turned into a beast, have you? A dwarf, a boar, a serpent. And this time a sheep – I wasn't expecting that! I don't know where you get these ideas.'

'And did you hear Monsieur Perrault's tale of "Cinderella" too? I thought it was rather wonderful.'

'Well, we know where he gets his ideas, off working women, that's where, and hardly crediting us. Oh, it had

97

some fine flourishes, but you know I'm old-fashioned – I think the fairy ought to live in an ash tree by her mother's grave, it's much more poetic. The stepsisters ought to be punished too. He just let them walk away! No doves! There ought to be doves at Cinderella's wedding, shouldn't there, my dears?'

'Yes!' Françoise agrees, bright with volatility. 'Birds should peck out their eyes!'

'His nurse mustn't have told it right,' Mimi says, her hand becoming a little beak, and pecking at Françoise's waist, so she squirms with delighted squeals. Marie is so glad she was able to employ Mimi, when she arrived back in Paris. She knew her old nurse would give her children the hugs they need, that she herself finds it hard to give. Her body stiffens, still, at touch, remembering what her mind won't. It often feels like a shard of ice is lodged in her heart.

'I think Monsieur Perrault was trying to add a little refinement to the tale,' Marie observes.

'You mean he's pompous,' Mimi pecks back, regarding, as she does, refinement as her enemy.

Belle-Belle the monkey has somehow got an eclair, and is eating it on the chandelier. 'There is some post, by the way,' the housemaid Berthe says, bringing in some letters – she is twenty and new, after the last girl married, and musical, often trilling songs softly to herself as she cleans. The dogs hurry in around her ankles and almost trip her up. One letter has a royal seal, that golden fleur-de-lis, and Madame d'Aulnoy is about to put it aside to read alone later, when she gives a little gasp: 'Oh!' For to her surprise, and private horror, it is not addressed to herself, but to her three daughters.

'Let me open it, let me,' Françoise cries, eyes always quick to spot her own name, tearing at it clumsily, her elder sisters peering over her shoulders in curiosity.

Inside is an invitation to the ball on thick, official paper.

Françoise screams with delight, then drags her copper-haired, eldest sister Judith into a spontaneous waltz. 'May I have this dance, madame,' she says in a silly low voice, making her lips smoochy.

'Do you think we ought to go, Mother?' Thérèse, her middle daughter, asks, so pale she often has shadows under her eyes, that solemn nose, something tamped down in her voice. 'If the king wants it?' What should Marie say?

No, daughters, I cannot keep you safe at Versailles. You must promise me to never leave this isle.

'It is hard to refuse His Majesty,' she replies, weakly.

Only half a mile away, in the shaken snow-globe that is Paris, Charles Perrault and Télésille are still trying to get home from the salon, waiting in their freezing carriage as a footman tries to dig it out of a snowdrift. Télésille is growing increasingly impatient, for those dozen letters are not going to write themselves before bedtime. 'I thought you were going to read your tale tonight,' Charles says to her. He helped her out earlier in the week with some notes on her first draft of 'The Discreet Princess'.

'As if – I couldn't go after Madame d'Aulnoy!' Télésille

declares, blushing. 'My goodness. How could I follow a writer of international reputation! Can you imagine? After Clio herself, the Muse of history!' (For this is Marie's 'salon' name, which has already appeared in the dedications of various poetry books, though she has never been heard to use it herself.) 'I'd rather the floor swallowed me!' Télésille adds, for good measure.

'You are too modest.'

'It's not modest to have the measure of your own gifts in the presence of greatness, cousin.' Her nose is stuffy with the cold and she blows it on a handkerchief of Genoese lace, producing a string of emeralds. 'Pardonne-moi. And I refer to your greatness too, of course, you were marvellous: the pumpkin and the mice! Adorable. You know I think these salons are second only to my great friend Sapho's Saturday Club,' Télésille adds.

As Télésille's face is sure to pop up at every single salon in Paris, her verdict might be considered a connoisseur's. Sapho is the salon name of the renowned bluestocking Mademoiselle de Scudéry, author of *Artamène ou le Grand Cyrus*, published in ten volumes, which at 1,954,300 words has the dubious distinction of being the longest novel ever written. Mademoiselle de Scudéry is also, as Télésille reminds everyone frequently, her very closest friend of all.

'The story of "The Ram" was delightful, I'll agree with that,' Charles says. He tries to avoid talking about Télésille's close friend Mademoiselle de Scudéry for the simple reason that he still hasn't got round to reading her novel.

The wine in his blood feels like some of the coral glow of the salon, still inside him. He keeps his fingers moving inside his leather gloves.

'Cousin, I meant to ask – I mean, this is delicate, but I know women, amongst themselves, talk of things that they may not in male company. I have to say I find myself intrigued by our hostess. The years after Madame d'Aulnoy's arrest – those missing years – do you have any idea what might have happened to her?'

'I believe she spent some time in Holland, England and Spain,' Télésille says. 'Didn't her mother go to England? And she is close friends with Saint-Évremond, is she not? He was in exile there at the time. I believe in Madrid she saw the bullfights and she once mentioned that the Spanish keep little sucking pigs as pets, as we do dogs, with collars of ribbon, and that everything was so stuffed with garlic, saffron and pepper she could hardly eat it. I shudder to think. She is a worldly woman.'

'Her children – guessing their ages. I couldn't help but speculate.'

'It's said she's had some great and tragic romances,' Télésille agrees.

'And how, I wonder, did she end up returning to Paris, given the warrant for her arrest?'

Télésille's eyebrows creep upwards like her face is a pot being filled. At last the lid bursts off. 'Well, that grande dame Philis, who used to attend the salon, God rest her soul, once told me that all Marie's charges were dropped because of "services to the Crown",' she loudly whispers. 'She thought Madame d'Aulnoy must have been a *spy*!'

'A spy?'

'Her mother's rumoured to be a spy too, apparently. I must admit the thought is thrilling.'

But Perrault is not happy to hear this. He is not sure why. Marie must have been spying for France, after all, and the country needs such brave men and women. It would explain how she was now allowed back in Paris, free from arrest, if she had bartered information for her liberty. Yet he realizes he gave away some private truths to her earlier; exposed his weakness. Did she entrap him into doing so? He has been a powerful man. He keeps a great many secrets. It meant something to him, talking to Madame d'Aulnoy so freely – in that moment, he thought, of shared understanding – but from now on he will have to be more careful and closed.

There is a sudden lurch. Their carriage starts to move again. 'Oh, thank goodness,' Télésille says. 'It's far too late for me, I must confess, and this journey is about my limit. Imagine travelling to Madrid! No, I am not a worldly woman, cousin. After such excitements there will be nothing finer than to be home, tucked up in my own cosy bed writing my correspondence. Fresh linen scented with lavender and a hot brick wrapped up in a flannel: that truly is the life!'

10. The Tale of the Pear

On account of their puny size and disappointing taste, in France wild pears are known as 'poires d'angoisse' or pears of anguish. In Versailles, though, in the kitchen garden, pears are bred for pleasure. Of the five hundred pear trees, the best usually fruit in January – the royal favourite, a type called 'Bon Chrétien d'Hiver', or 'Good Christian of Winter'. Each pear is very large – the blossom end engorged, the eye deeply sunk – whilst the skin is a finely grained pale yellow, with a red blush on the side that has been touched by the sunlight. It is known for its brittle, lightly scented, almost translucent flesh that drips with a sugary juice; that soaks your mouth when your teeth sink into it. The gardener here, Jean-Baptiste de La Quintinie, says that when a pear is ripe its neck yields to the touch and smells slightly of wet roses.

This winter they have not ripened, though, but have frozen to solid gold. Murders of crows sit on the branches of the pear trees, pecking at the rime of them. They have become fairy fruit; those dangling impossibilities. What would you give to taste one?

11. The Tale of the Frog

Spring always comes, though. Is it not magic? The world's deep magic.

March brings the vast respite of thaw, that huge unburdening, that gentling – all winter's knives and jaws turning soft and blunt; little chunks of ice riding off on their own giddy melt; everything dripping and plipping and making little streams and rivulets; tender pellucid fingers feeling their way towards the sea; all the tiny busywork.

And with the returning sun, too, sex. Tulips, first found as wild flowers in Central Asia – named for the Persian word 'tulipan', for turban – thrust and bow in the warm soil of Versailles, their variegated 'broken' petals licked with carmine flames. The early worm-catchers begin their chorus, skylarks and song thrushes courting at dawn. Catkins dangle like soft, tiny pairs of elven stockings. Fairy-sized wigs appear on the pussy willows. Hawthorn and sloe put on their powder and patches, to catch a bee's eye.

The heart of a frozen frog can stop beating, but as it thaws it will flicker back to life. This pair of bronze frogs in the pond seem to spoon, the male grasping the female's forelegs, his eyes glazed with instinct, spraying sperm over her eggs as they slide into the water: a jellified clump of crystal balls.

Another hops on to the dusty path, where the Princesse de Conti picks him up. He is supple with mucus. 'Ugh,' she says. 'You're a greasy little prince. No kisses off me.' She spills him back into the pond. 'Go on, spunk in there.'

The Princesse de Conti is on heat. This morning she rode out hunting – cutting a dash in her riding gear of a man's jacket and black silk breeches – only to find the friction of the horse between her thighs felt almost dangerous, like she might black out with pleasure, so slick and sensitive is she down there. There is plenty of cock available, of course, but that is not what she is wet for. Her slimy husband has been a disaster in bed since their wedding night, and they have no offspring.

Lately, men turn her stomach even; she simply has no appetite for them. She blames her parents. Not that they have spent much time getting to know her. The princess passed her childhood at arm's length from Versailles. Madame de Maintenon, then a governess, brought the princess up with her other bastard siblings in that secret house on the Rue de Vaugirard. Although officially she's been legitimized now, the sense of shame has never quite gone away, and she feels her presence at court is tolerated, at best – Athénaïs only taking her aside occasionally to tell her to make more of herself and quit smoking. Still, she can hardly avoid the grotesque, ongoing drama of Louis and Athénaïs's relationship, given ballads have been written about it across the continent. The princess's whole personality has been constructed in opposition to that of her biological mother, who repulses her: so needy, thickly made-up, feminine, sickly-sweet. Ugh. All those desperate, perpetual, little machinations to lure her father into Athénaïs's parlour! The endless, evil stratagems the king's erections now require!

Nor does it help that her father has been suffering from a painful sphincter and – after many torturous attempts by Fagon to make it feel better, involving a red-hot poker and rose petals soaked in Burgundy wine – was finally diagnosed with an anal fistula. After developing a new instrument, the royal probe (and killing several patients of lesser blood in practice), the surgeon Felix finally operated successfully, a fact that all of France now apparently celebrates. According to the paper, *Le Mercure galant*, it has been declared 'L'année de la Fistule'. Half his male courtiers have started sashaying round with their buttocks swaddled in homage. Baboons, she thinks. Men make themselves so vile.

There is a fairy tale she remembers from the salon, about a prince with a huge nose, and the courtiers who pull their children's noses each morning to make them longer.

It is Madame de Murat she wants. Henriette. How Henriette has avoided her these last few weeks, but how it has made her hunger grow. She is ravenous for Henriette. She wants to bite that throat. Taste that cunt on her fingers. God *damn* it!

Drink usually takes the edge off. She will go inside, play some cards, drink some wine. A big glass of red. Yesterday she drank too much, and – as the palace memoirists will surely later write – rendered in all directions the wines she swallowed. No, she must do something about Henriette, but what? There is a salon at Marie's house again this week, if she could only get a note to her. That's it, she will write her a letter. The kind a libertine might write in a novel, as an instrument of seduction.

The Princesse de Conti makes her way to her apartment, past the sphinxes and bowers and innumerable gardeners, plunging into the cool shade of the palace. Past the chapel; past the goat being milked beside a painting of Juno. At last, she pours the wine, lights up her pipe and sits at her desk. Dips her pen into the ink.

Dear Henriette,

Some say the day begins with God, but I began today, as every day, by thinking of the object of my love, for I think of her incessantly. On the hunt I thought of you, for there is no thrill in killing any more, when I only want to finish you – my white deer – and feel the throes of your little death closing round my fingers. When I bring myself to pleasure, I picture your eyes sliding back in your head – your hiss like a death-rattle.

I am writing to you, most cruel sister, because although this evening you will be close enough that I might touch that tender white throat, or the small of your back, or your fingers, which I tremble to think of – that fist they made inside me – I will not be able to touch you, and it is to me an agony. I cannot stand to wait any longer to know my fate, and whether I have been cast out from that bliss that is your arms forever. Are you afraid?

Is it your soul you fear for? Have you read the Greek philosopher Plato's theory of love? He believes love is composed of a single soul inhabiting two bodies. Zeus cut us in half, tearing us apart – and well I feel that your soul and mine were mingled once. I have wandered the earth through many lives to find you again, Henriette, I cannot lose you now! It is my destiny, I am sure of it, to weave my limbs with yours, to kiss you endlessly, everywhere, always.

My darling, I can think of nothing but that I am madly in love with you. If you know this and refuse me, then you are so cruel one should not love you, but I cannot help myself. Please come in my carriage again or promise to meet me – send me a sign – for you are both the fever consuming me and its cure.

Always,
Your Princess

It is a fine letter, she decides, in which she has truly brought out her inner Lothario. Extremely erotic. Romantic, even. And perhaps it is even true, she thinks, as the ink dries – the writing a revelation – perhaps I really am in love with her! The wax makes a single, molten drip to seal the envelope, red as a bitten lip. When this is done, the Princesse de Conti takes to her bed and masturbates, before finding her chambermaid and enquiring how she may discreetly procure a dildo.

12. The Tale of the Subtle Princess

Angélique arrives at the salon early, Madame Miaou under her arm.

Madame d'Aulnoy is arranging flowers around the parlour: armfuls of irises, peonies and narcissi for spring in porcelain vases. Her daughters help her. They went to the ball last month, and it was fine, absolutely fine. They looked so pretty in their dresses – gold, silver and sky blue for Françoise – and only danced with little boys, children really, and drank lemonade. 'The king told Thérèse she reminded him of someone,' Françoise reported, which the girls thought was probably flattering, but otherwise little had happened, which Marie was very glad of.

The girls coo over the cat. Madame Miaou has such a luxurious little face: milky eyes like bluish opal, fine whiskers trembling on her cheeks and brows that seem always to have sunlight caught in them; the clean tongue like a scrap of pink silk. She is softer than mink when you tickle her. And Angélique too, Marie d'Aulnoy thinks, herself puts her in mind of a fine white cat, wanting only to stretch out in some puddle of sun or nibble treats from your palm; to be stroked until she purrs.

'So lovely to see you, Angélique,' Marie says. 'Berthe, please ask Anne at once to prepare drinking chocolate and the violet box of sweetmeats; we'll take them in the garden before the salon begins.'

'Yes, madame.'

'Is that all right?' Angélique asks. 'I didn't wish to bother you, it's only . . .'

'Of course, it's no bother, I'm nearly ready here. Come, let's go and sit beneath the magnolia, it's quite lovely.'

'Now, what is the matter?' Marie asks, once they are sat down under the flowers, proffering the violet box. Angélique takes a bonbon, cracks the chocolate with her teeth and feels liqueur spurt into her mouth.

'It's my husband, Claude,' she says, swallowing. 'Oh, Marie, I think I've made such a terrible mistake with him. He's been travelling, you know, and so I've been living very much as before and just putting him out of my mind, although I have needs of course – a woman wants to be told she's beautiful when she puts on a new dress, by a man I mean. And a woman wants to be touched, doesn't she? I need my hugs, I'm just that sort of person, Marie. I mean, you must miss that, right?'

Marie's mouth closes on nothing, then opens again, as if waiting for itself to do something – she avoids questions about her private feelings as she might a flame. But fortunately, very quickly, they come to the mutual realization that Angélique does not genuinely want an answer, only a nod of reassurance, which Marie supplies – other people's inner selves are a drain on the world's attention that Angélique has always found difficult to bear.

'But I've been managing,' she continues. 'And I was

looking forward to him coming home from Venice this week, I thought he might have some little treats for me – you know they have the loveliest glass in Murano, Burano lace, masks, marble paper, and those little yellow butter cookies – and I put on a new dress and perfume, and this adorable little patch by my mouth like a black heart, worn at the corner, à la coquette, trying to be cute for him, you know. I miss my mother, actually. You know she wasn't the greatest mother in many ways but she always used to dress me up like a little doll, and I used to feel like I was the cutest girl in the whole wide world. Anyway he came back and, oh, Marie. He didn't even want to touch me. I reached for his arm and he flinched back like he didn't even want to – to spit on me.' She starts to weep.

'Oh, my darling Angélique, I'm so sorry,' Madame d'Aulnoy says.

'Like I was just an old hag—'

'You're gorgeous, Angélique. We all think you're gorgeous.'

'And then he asked me for money. For some of my allowance! But it's been running through my hands this year, the prices of everything have gone up, so the valet, Moura, tells me, but he's honest, I do trust him – I don't know what I'd do without him, he's a lamb. And the king expects us to spend money on French lace and these ball-dresses all the time, you have to keep up appearances, and well – Claude didn't even say what he needed it for!'

'Do you have any idea, though? Has he got into debt, do you think?'

'I thought he was rich, Marie. That's why I married him! You know, I've always worried about men only wanting me for my income. All those adventurers. But he had lots of money, or he seemed to – he told my aunt he had a large fortune. You know he gave me the most extravagant bouquet of flowers once, studded with diamonds, and he said there's plenty more where that came from, I swear to God. And I like jewels. What woman doesn't like a bit of sparkle? But also, I felt – who doesn't want to be spoiled, right? But also: I thought, he isn't after my money. He can look after himself. He just wants me. He used to say I had the most darling dimple. And now I feel like such a fool, Marie. He called me—'

'It's all right.'

'A washed-up old lush,' she chokes out. 'I don't even drink wine before lunchtime, Marie!'

'Well just don't give him the money, then. That's not how you ask for favours. You say you trust Moura? Keep him close. Ask him to guard your door at night if need be. Do you think you might be able to get the marriage annulled?'

'The thing is I've had a source of comfort these last few months,' Angélique says, lip trembling, tickling her cat's stomach with its eight nipples, like cherry-blossom buds. 'Well all right, two. There was this captain in the king's guards, very dishy, and then this other young man you might know – well he's lost a lot of interest, he's not called for days, and it just makes me feel ancient suddenly. I looked in the mirror this morning and I was like, my God, your skin looks like a piece of paper a child has played with.'

'Versailles is full of young men like that, Angélique, you're not the one that's disposable,' Marie reassures her friend, assuming she's talking about Briou, although she does feel – for the slightest moment – a twinge of compassion for Claude; the sense that he may have his own side to tell in this tale. Angélique's inheritance, after all, is not some innate moral quality, and his fortune may have changed for as yet unexplained reasons, as fortunes do.

'Anyway, the thing is, Claude says he's going to ask for a lettre de cachet because of my infidelities. He says if I don't give him the money, he'll have me locked up, Marie! And I don't know how he *knows*.' This is more serious, and any thought of empathy with Claude's perspective immediately dissipates. Wealthy women in France at this time are often locked up for male convenience: palmed off on convents, imprisoned or exiled. A lettre de cachet is a secret order from the king, who is quite the gaoler. Madame d'Aulnoy recalls the click of the lock all those years ago with a shudder; how she tried to calm her bawling newborn, walking her round and round in that turret's small stone room.

'He snatched the jewels off my throat to pawn, I swear to God. Look—'

There's a red mark on Angélique's throat, where Claude pulled them tight. Madame d'Aulnoy gets a cold feeling when she looks at it, like prescience:

snow   white   rose   red   snow   white

'You must try and stay safe, Angélique. Perhaps it's for the best, to put such dalliances aside for now . . .'

Though they have much to discuss, the arrival of other guests is announced and they must make their way back inside to the salon, Angélique popping into Marie's bedroom to redo her powder and tear-streaked rouge.

Charles and Télésille have arrived first, only to be greeted by Marie's daughters – who Charles insists on being introduced to individually, memorizing their names ('And do any of you intend to become fairies like your mother?') – and the monkey showing her teeth. The Princesse de Conti arrives next, swaggering in with her letter to Henriette rolled up in her pouch.

Marie's old friend Saint-Évremond is in town, to her delight, and brings the elderly authoress and courtesan Ninon de l'Enclos. Saint-Évremond has an odd swelling on his forehead, like the stub of a horn between his brows, which makes him look like a beast in a silk shirt. 'It has been too long!' he tells Marie. 'But I am always so very happy to see you at the heart of literary Paris, where you belong. These contes de fées are still the talk of the city.'

'The years have flown,' she says. 'But you look just the same, dear friend.'

'I'm not sure that is a compliment, Marie, but I will take it so. Everything hurts these days, but I don't complain. It well becomes a man who is no longer young to forget that he ever was.'

Others arrive too for the first time, providing further proof that the salon's reputation is rising: the Duchess of Nemours makes her entrance, followed by Henriette, running late, who has brought a male cousin (an excuse not to be alone with me, the Princesse de Conti thinks, irritated, although she will not lose faith in the power of her letter).

Anne is handing out pineapple sherbets, in honour of the warmer weather, whilst Mimi wrangles the monkey, with her ancient, shrunken face and wild white side-burns. ('Belle-Belle! Out! Shoo!')

'My compliments to the cook,' Perrault tells Anne, after devouring a zinging spoonful. 'More delights from your kitchen! A tropical reverie! All of us envy your mistress, dear woman, to have such a marvel as you.' Anne, not good at taking compliments, bows her sleek silver head and hurries on, like one of the greyhounds.

'Shall we begin, then?' Marie asks the bustling room.

'But – but Briou!' Angélique exclaims, fluttering slightly as she tries to swallow so many emotions all at once. 'What shall we do for a prince without him?'

'And Charlotte isn't here yet,' Télésille says. 'I saw her at Saint-Sulpice just this Sunday with her mother and father, and she definitely said she was coming today. She says she has a new story, about a princess trapped in a turret, and a prince falls in love with her, and—'

Everyone in the room, of course, knows how stories operate: circumstance, actions, consequences. They quickly do the narrative work, and find themselves picturing the same thing: Love's Young Dream. Charlotte-Rose and Briou, kissing.

'Oh,' Télésille says, embarrassed by the knowledge

dawning in twin sunrises on her cheeks. 'Um. But maybe she's not well, though. The tree pollen does affect me so at this time of year, don't you find? *Achoo*. There I go. Pardon me, blithering.'

'Télésille,' Marie d'Aulnoy says. 'You promised us we might be so fortunate as to hear your debut tale today – I hope you can confirm this happy news that you are joining our group of Modern Fairies, Les Fées Modernes! Might you be so kind as to begin our evening?'

'Oh no,' Télésille says. 'That's too much of an honour, surely.'

'Not at all, the honour is all ours. Why, your debut is sure to go down in literary history! Do tell us, friend, what your tale is called.'

'"The Subtle Princess",' Télésille admits.

'Bravo, I like the sound of her already,' the Princesse de Conti observes, taking a drag of her pipe.

So, Marie-Jeanne L'Héritier de Villandon, known by ourselves as Télésille, begins her story 'The Subtle Princess' – or 'The Discreet Princess', as it is sometimes translated – which really is an extraordinarily memorable one, as Marie d'Aulnoy predicts. It will later be collected in her book *Ingenious Medleys* of 1697, soon after she has attained the great prestige of being the first woman elected to one of the exclusive French academies, in Toulouse, and established as one of the nine Muses by the Ricovrati of Padua. If you share my own taste, you will perhaps find it finer than her tale 'The Robe of Sincerity', that rather priggish and convoluted story which seems to prefigure 'The Emperor's New Clothes', with its robe that displays images of virtuous women such as Penelope only if its wearer is virginal. But it must also be admitted that, in this moment, the company find the tale quite startling.

It is about a girl called Finessa who has two elder sisters: idle Nonchalante, who wanders around at all hours in her dressing gown and slippers, and Babillarde, known for her itch to prattle. Their mother has died, and their father, a king, needs to travel so, to best protect their virtue, he decides to lock all three in a castle. Each is given a magic distaff made of glass that will shatter if their virtue fails.

However, his enemy's son, a virile young man called Richcraft, is on the prowl. Disguised as a beggarwoman, he dupes Nonchalante and Babillarde into letting him within the castle. Then, revealing himself as a prince, he flatters, makes promises of marriage, and, inevitably, causes their distaffs to shatter.

'The world is full of such dupes,' Télésille notes, as all the room – surely – think grave thoughts about the state of Charlotte-Rose's virtue.

But Finessa is different. When he steps near her, she toys with her axe as if it is 'a delicate fan'. She promises him a soft bed then builds one over a scaffold that drops him several hundred feet into the castle's filthy drains, with the slops and faeces.

Still, her sisters are now pregnant by him, and Richcraft returns, circling, hungry for vengeance. Knowing the sisters crave fruit, he leaves baskets of sweet plums and apricots outside. They beg Finessa to fetch them,

117

only for Richcraft to trap her. He shows Finessa a barrel lined with razors, smashed glass and knives, threatening to roll her in it from a great height. But as he gloats, she kicks him inside instead, then pushes him down the mountain.

Later, furious to be dying from his own evil plan, Richcraft makes his brother, Belavoir, promise to marry Finessa then stab her to death on their wedding night. When his two newborns are brought to his chamber, their ear-splitting cries finish him off.

Now Belavoir is actually in love with Finessa but, promises to brothers being more important than mere women, he prepares to kill her. Fortunately, Finessa has put a dummy in her bed. It is made of a bale of straw, some animal entrails and a bladder full of sheep's blood. After he stabs the dummy and looks really very sorry about the mess, they live happily ever after.

'Well, apart from Nonchalante,' Télésille concludes, 'who is given work as a punishment and dies of vex- ation, and Babillarde, who breaks her skull trying to escape the castle. The end.'

There is a long moment of silence.

'Well,' says the Princesse de Conti, exhaling.

'My dear Télésille,' Henriette says, releasing the ten- sion with a laugh. 'You are positively bloodthirsty. Who knew such dark, twisted scenarios were playing out behind your genial exterior? I was expecting something pious, yet you contrive to have the prince fall into shit! I would like to see more stories where men fall into sewers. Perhaps I will follow you in this new craze.'

'Bravo,' says Perrault, beginning to clap in order to remind the others to do so. They join in at last, coming back to themselves. 'Very dramatic, cousin! And the bed trick! In Basile's version I believe the dummy is sweet pastry, so he weeps with regret over the sweet fragrance of his beloved, does he not? But a sheep's bladder filled with blood, well well. Quite a different effect.'

'It was not too much, cousin?' Télésille asks, suddenly doubting her artistic decisions. 'Oh, it was too much, wasn't it? I was aiming for a simple, rustic feel, and such stories fill with impurities as they pass through the mouths of common people, as water does when it passes through a dirty culvert – but you think I was too coarse for this esteemed company?'

'Not at all,' Madame d'Aulnoy says, who makes it a rule to treat debutantes at her salon with kindness. 'We were rapt! What a gift to take the room's breath like that. And it's so funny to have Richcraft die of listening to his own screaming baby!'

'Many men have expired in similar circumstances,' Henriette's cousin observes, who has twelve children and looks rather haggard himself.

'I blame the father,' the Princesse de Conti notes. 'Locking up his daughters with glass distaffs, the whole tragedy was inevitable.' She is thinking of her dildo, which has arrived, but also of how foolish it is, this tiresome obsession with female purity when the impure are so much better in bed. Who does it serve except the frigid? Untouched old Télésille, having nightmares about wedding nights and her razor-filled cunt, sorry, barrel.

More stories follow. Henriette has written something called 'The Fortunate Punishment' involving a dog called Blanc-Blanc and a bridge of white roses, but the Princesse de Conti finds it hard to concentrate on anything except how to slip the letter into Henriette's fingers. As the highest-ranking person there it is usual for her to sit, but even princesses must relieve themselves sometimes – or might she step towards the window once the story ends, as if to admire that gold of the early-evening light over Paris, that has illumined the candlestick of the magnolia?

Henriette finishes her tale with a wedding. 'Though I will not attempt a description of it,' she explains, with a wry smile. 'For however agreeable to the lovers themselves, a wedding is almost always a dull affair to the general company.'

At this there is great laughter. 'No one ends a story half as well as you, Henriette,' Marie is saying. 'You are the wittiest of us all.'

The Princesse de Conti stands with a lightness of head. She has drunk a great deal of wine today – more than two bottles – and will drink more again. Gently reeling, she begins to cross the jostling room, towards Henriette: her cool white forearms, long brown eyes in that fierce, sharp little face. *I will be a subtle princess*, she thinks. *The discreet princess*. She is pushing her fingers eagerly into the pouch on her belt, but then she registers with shock an emptiness. No, she is being foolish, surely. Her hand digs in deeper, as she glances back at the carpet, the chair, but it has gone: her love letter is no longer there.

13. The Tale of Bearskin

It is late at Versailles, beneath the pink paper lanterns that glow throughout the gardens. Fountains dance in the grove. That scent of a thousand tuberoses; in the distance the splash of people fooling around on gondolas; someone playing the harp. In the sky, the breadcrumb trails of the stars. Even the owl hoots, as if for ambience.

After too much champagne, Charlotte-Rose de La Force has fallen asleep in Briou's lap beneath a gold-cloth pavilion. It is not, really, like they have many other places to go. There are so many nobles to pack into the north wing that their rooms are chopped into tiny units with no windows, or give on to dismal interior wells. Charlotte-Rose has ended up in one of the meanest, with a servant sleeping in her wardrobe.

No, he is glad for them to rest here, at leisure. He breathes her in.

They have had a wonderful night. When the monk Dom Pérignon first created champagne, the legend is that he cried out: 'Come quickly, I am tasting the stars!' Tonight, Briou has drunk stars too. They have had such fun, dancing and gambling – she kissed his die for luck, which worked. And Charlotte-Rose is gorgeous, which also helps, all his mates slapping him on the back – 'Get in there, Briou'; 'Well played, my man'. He felt a growing sense of confidence this evening, particularly as they watched the fireworks whilst she toyed with his hand, that he is sure to take her virginity. He will deflower her, which is a thing that he is definitely supposed to be excited to do. The thought makes him let out a giddy giggle. Briou thinks of those words of Don Juan in Molière's play: 'As for me, beauty embraces me wherever I find it, and I can easily yield to the sweet violence with which it sweeps me along.' He imagines it as this: a sweet violence, and himself a new Don Juan.

Her head is so beautiful. Perfect really. The slightest flush, like on a petal. The little drowsy mouth, a bubble caught in it. A curl of hair on her brow, just so. It feels entirely different from being with the other women, being with her.

Briou feels his own eyes begin to close too. His chin creeps towards his neck, as his head lolls forward. As he begins to dream his cock hardens. Charlotte-Rose's unconscious head slumps against it, her soft face, like a stone rolling over the entrance to a cave of treasure.

He begins to rock, ever so gently, against her cheek-bone, his cock under the silk breeches near that breathing mouth, the neat teeth. The pressure begins to build, to thicken; the vague, dizzying feeling gaining mass, like a thunderstorm accumulating inside him. The animal in him winning: the wolf, the rearing serpent.

Then suddenly he jerks awake. Where is he? Charlotte? Oh, she is on his lap. Snow White who will wake with a kiss. He really should do that. Or she is Sleeping Beauty and he is lopping through the tangle of roses to get to her, hacking, closer closer to her body untouched for a hundred years: his alone, to possess, to touch. Oh God. He cannot stop himself, closer closer, he will have his happy ending – he is about to come – oh! oh!

Then she wakes up. 'Briou?' she says, as though she doesn't quite recognize his face, its dumb-beast look, his panting breath. 'Briou? What on earth are you doing?'

And he kisses Charlotte-Rose then, in panic, because he cannot speak – pulling her up in his arms, his tongue thrusting inside her mouth, in the French manner, as he orgasms almost painfully, silently. Sperm spurts in awful jets into his breeches; he jerks like he is in a carriage juddering over rocks.

Her mouth tastes oddly of citrus.

'Oh,' she says afterwards, confused. Was that the kiss of true love? It was certainly intense, though not quite as delicate as she was expecting, and certainly wetter. 'Goodness, that was— Oh, Briou, you really like me?'

'I can't stay,' he blurts, feeling the cool seep through his breeches like bells ringing for midnight. He stands up in alarm.

'You can't go *now*!' she yelps, for this is the moment of her life. Is he kidding?

'Marry me,' he splutters, impulsively – or almost, perhaps, out of politeness. For this is part of the script – is it not? – which boys, no less than girls, learn on the knee.

'Of course I will!' she cries out in delight. 'Oh, Charles! Oh, Charles, I'm so happy!' She looks suddenly as if she means to embrace him, so he holds her face instead – at a slight distance – and leans over for a soft but careful peck. Her dreamy little face. And though he realizes he has not quite acquitted himself as the new Don Juan, the young man, it must be said, does not immediately regret what he has done. Recklessness can be a fine and enlivening sensation. He knows his father's fury will be completely off the scale, yet Briou can also feel a story beginning – which is to say, the energy of destruction coursing through him.

So it is that, just three days later, they marry. It is a simple, hasty wedding, but once he decides to do something Briou is an impatient boy, brought to temper by waiting. His father has been pressing him for an answer about the Spanish sourpuss, and this is his answer. Let's see how his father likes this diplomacy; how he answers this move! His father is also away, of course, at the family castle, and the thing is best brought off in his absence. Besides, for Briou, as for many a Mother Goose, such adventures conclude in the marriage bed. He has not thought beyond it; is perhaps hormonally incapable. Sexual intercourse with Charlotte-Rose – youthful, desirable, valuable, unblemished Charlotte-Rose – is his focus; the end towards which his whole self now blunders.

'It cannot be, though, Briou! Your family will keep us apart, surely? My dowry is too small, I'm too poor for you,' Charlotte-Rose says the night before, sensibly, covering her mole with her hand as if it were her poverty, trying to stamp out her own kindling excitement.

'Love doesn't care about money,' Briou replies, really impressing himself with his own turn of phrase. Perhaps he will be a poet after all.

And things proceed, rapidly, shockingly. The king's permission is sought; a signature obtained; Charlotte lets her family and the Dauphine believe she will be attending Marie's salon that night; vows are spoken in a small ceremony – all a blur, a total blur – before they are in the apartment, his friend's, which he has borrowed for the night, and there is nothing for it but to strip her: the chemise, the boned stays, the stomacher, stockings, garters. It takes so long – so many clothes! But Briou very much feels that she is worth it: we must give him this. For Briou is mildly hysterical with desire; aglow with it; unable to stop laughing aloud to himself, even, at what he is about to be permitted to do. He kisses his wife's nipples with an awestruck trembling reverence, her body the most magnificent thing he has ever seen.

Charlotte-Rose lies with her head tilted, so that he will see the left side of her face at this moment, from which she thinks her nose looks less crooked, whilst sucking in her stomach. As he pushes himself into her, the feeling is everything Briou hopes: he thinks of an exquisite fur slipper that is the perfect fit. 'I love you,' he groans. 'Oh, I love you, I love you, I love you, Charlotte-Rose!' For Charlotte-Rose, on the other hand, the experience, it has to be admitted, is something of a disappointment.

That night in the apartment, as her husband sleeps, satiated, beside her, she stares up at the ceiling in a daze. Having crept out and sponged her bits with vinegar, as is apparently the practice, now she cannot get to sleep. From other women's conversation, she has understood that it is not only the man who feels pleasure between the sheets. And so, her husband never having pretended to lack experience, she was expecting great things from this occasion: a whole new room of extraordinary sensation was to be unlocked within her, marriage being the necessary key. She had thought a little glimpse of such thrills was afforded her when Briou touched the instep of her foot in Madame d'Aulnoy's salon. But sexual intercourse has not, for her, replicated any such moment of exquisite sensitivity, but rather filled her, as he noisily laboured, with a grim sense of nothing much at all. After the first sting of entry, Charlotte-Rose was not, in truth, even certain if he was in the room or out of it, as it were, half the time.

Is this it? she wonders. Is it for this, truly, that all those quests are undertaken? All those curses and spindles and frogs and thorns and balls, for this?

However, it is not yet over, quite. There are still obstacles to come. The next morning, after Charlotte-Rose gets up an hour before him, tiptoeing to the dressing table and putting on her patches and powders so he will not see her without her make-up, Briou leaves to attend the king's getting-up ceremony, whilst Charlotte-Rose has to wait upon the Dauphine. By evening, when she searches for him in the usual places, she is told by one of his friends in the Grand Appartement that Briou's father arrived at court, flung his son rather roughly into a carriage, then announced he was taking him to the family castle until they receive confirmation that the marriage has been annulled.

'You wouldn't kiss my die, would you?' the friend asks,

sipping his Armagnac rather lasciviously. 'Seems to have worked for your husband, lucky man.'

'I fail to see why he's lucky,' Charlotte-Rose snaps. 'Being separated from his true love!'

There's laughter, then. That's when she begins to realize this is serious. She has been deflowered. She has lost her value, cheapened herself, and for it received such scant recompense! Every hope she's ever had for her life is over. She'll just be a lady-in-waiting forever, won't she, and a sullied one at that – the subject of gossipy asides and pitying looks? Well, she doesn't see why she should take it. Charlotte-Rose has read enough secret histories for a romantic plan to form in her mind.

So it is that she takes a carriage to the castle. And she finds, on her arrival – I know this is scarcely believable, but you must trust me, everything I tell you now is true – that a group of performers have arrived in town: there are acrobats, a jester, musicians, a travelling menagerie of monkeys and bears. A man juggles in the square. When Charlotte-Rose asks him, he tells her they are going to the castle tomorrow for a grand ball – there'll be a great feast and candles will be lit in the moat. 'I must get in there,' Charlotte cries. Her only currency, of course, is fashion – she offers him her open-work bracelet set with opals and her best fan, though it is painful for her to part with both. He eyes her wedding ring. 'No,' she says, 'please not that,' thinking *not yet*.

'All right,' the juggler agrees. 'I'll do you a favour. But you might not like my plan that much, though, a girl that likes looking pretty. You'll need a disguise, won't you?

We have a bearskin I reckon I could put you under, if you care to walk with the dancing bears, you know – trot in like a little upright mammal. What do you think, my sweet angel?'

And now Charlotte-Rose is walking into the castle, under her bearskin, head down and paws up. The pelt is incredibly hot and itchy, and may even have a flea or two nestled in its thick fur. And she is scared and tired, and knows really – of course she does – that her marriage will be annulled; that Briou will give her up; that one day, when she is old and grey, she will look back at herself in this moment and shake her head, full of grief for this hopeful self. But still, damn it, right now she is the girl in the story. She really is. She is the girl in the fucking fairy tale.

14. The Tale of the Witch

The hulking bridge of the Pont Neuf above the Seine is one of the great symbols of the city. Whilst its stony gargoyles watch over the river's flow, crowds cross and clog above them: peddlers, booksellers, dog-barbers, tooth-pullers, actors, jugglers. This evening it is quieter than usual, for the city is hissing and squalling with rain, but the chief of police – Gabriel Nicolas de La Reynie – is there, listening intently to a figure wearing a loup. The black velvet mask renders the speaker's visage eerily immobile, but for the glistening, darting eyeballs. Were you one of the cutpurses who famously work the bridge, stealing gentlemen's cloaks and pocket watches, perhaps you could creep close enough to overhear a strange narrative: a picaresque containing princesses, enchantments, talking birds, pitchers filled with tears, ogres, wishing trees. A Palace of Voluptuousness and a Palace of Revenge. Reynie's lip hardens into a curl as his spy speaks, then he hands them a bag heavy with coins and turns briskly, in the direction of Charles Perrault's house.

Louis XIV imported hundreds of costly white swans to add elegance to the Seine, but only a few have not been struck down or poisoned by the filthy, congested river. As is his habit, Reynie checks on their nest as he passes – a couple of ugly cygnets have survived from the latest clutch – then plunges into the famous streets of Paris: ones on which luxury and poverty exist cheek by jowl. On every corner there are signs of modernity – construction sites, postboxes, public carriages, hairdressers. A whore stands, dripping, in front of a row of boutiques, their gleaming shop windows displaying luxury goods: perfumes, artificial flowers, stockings, Chinese silks. A foreign tourist, caught out by the weather, consults his guidebook. Abandoned on a doorstep, a baby howls at the sky.

During the Fronde, when the nobles rebelled – in those days of the twelve hundred barricades, the fighting on the streets – young Louis XIV had to flee Paris. Since then, the king has distrusted Parisians, himself coming into the city as little as possible, and he made Reynie his chief of police in order to keep Paris under control. It is a role that Reynie was surely destined for. Every day, he imposes order on this chaotic city: Paris owes him its street lights, its pavements, its parking rules.

Reynie has taken to heart, too, that line in Molière's *Tartuffe* – 'We live under a king who hates deceit / A king whose eyes see into every heart.' He has installed a network of paid informers he calls his 'flies' – amongst all ranks of person, from vagabonds to royal bastards – dirty little telltales he loathes, but who allow him a certain omniscience on Louis's behalf. Like some dark angel, he prides himself on seeing into every little crack of this city; beyond the chain of each closed street; into every house seven storeys high, dim and crowded; every inn; every rag-picker's hovel.

'In the service of Caesar, everything is legitimate.' That one's the tragedian, Pierre Corneille. Louis likes that line as well. And another: 'I would not like a king who would obey.'

Reynie is capable of benevolence – did he not build thirty ovens in Paris this winter, to bake bread for the poor? But they still shoved and rioted, of course, selfish with hunger. And he is happier as a vengeful God. Paris used to have a place they called 'the Courtyard of Miracles' – so many of its residents were miraculously 'cured' of their feigned blindness or lameness when they got home each evening. It was a ghastly city of sin, half-buried in mud; roof-tiles slipping. It smelt of beggars and cutpurses pissing themselves; boiling bones. A city of barefoot little ghosts and burning demons, pustular with syphilis and gin. But one day he gathered a hundred and fifty soldiers together and, under a barrage of rocks, they tore the whole place down. Just razed it to the ground. The bad spirits simply left. He has never felt such clarity of purpose as he did that day.

He strolls swiftly on through the fierce spring rain, head down, past a bronze statue of Louis. Perhaps he should have hired a private sedan chair – the stinking gruel of the road is splashing his robe, and Reynie is a fastidious man – but he always finds he thinks more clearly whilst walking. An onlooker might say that Reynie has a sensual face, with his heavy-lidded eyes, and that mouth like an expensive little cushion under his moustache, but his only real pleasure is breaking bad news. How good he feels, as he slowly releases it: the drip-drip.

The corner of his mouth is twisting upwards with anticipated joy as he raps on Perrault's door, with its weighty, ornate knocker. He is a tall man, who has to stoop at most doors, broad and big-handed, yet his movements are measured and neat.

'Reynie,' Perrault says, startled, wigless, flinching slightly. He is wearing his robe de chambre, a kind of dressing gown. 'What a surprise this is! It's been some time.' He has been sat at the table with his son, Pierre, helping him with his Latin by the oil lamp. Now, as he invites Reynie in, he chivvies his son upstairs. 'Please take a seat. Can I get you some refreshments?'

'Could I wash my hands, do you mind?' Reynie asks.

'Of course, of course.' Perrault helps his guest to find the washstand, then orders his valet to make tea. No one desires a visit from Reynie exactly, although there may be many good reasons for him to drop by – over the last decade they collaborated quite extensively on Louis's plans to make the city a New Rome; there is much business that they might discuss. 'Sit by the fire to dry out, Reynie. It is a wet, wet night.'

'You're back in Paris,' Reynie says, taking off his hat. 'You must miss Versailles already. The clean air. The lack of human misery.'

'Paris is a – a marvellous city,' Perrault replies. 'And much to your credit. The City of Lights, they call it now, thanks to your innovations! I have plenty to occupy me here – my brother is around, his colonnade of the Louvre is superb, is it not? The Academy. And the Comédie-Française is opening, whilst it fills me with a certain pride to walk in the Tuileries, of course – to think the first manned hydrogen balloon took flight from there! It is a place of marvels.'

'I wonder if you and I are breathing the same foul air,' Reynie says, shaking his head. 'I have a sensitive nose, Perrault, and Paris stinks. I cannot get the smell off me at night, however much I scrub: garlic, rotten teeth and chamber pots.'

'I suppose I am used to it.'

Reynie looks around himself, ponderously, taking it in. 'No engravings of the king on your walls, Charles?'

'I am redecorating shortly.'

'You were at the theatre last night.'

'I was?' Perrault replies. He was, but how does Reynie know? He took his sons to see Molière's new play, *The Clever Women* – another attack on bluestockings, it turned out; the man really has it in for ladies who read – and was startled to realize that one of the characters in it, the pompous Trissotin, was based on the Abbé Cotin so precisely that they used his poem about a lavender-coloured coach from *Gallant Verse* verbatim. An audience member even whispered that the actor playing Trissotin had filched the abbé's actual coat to wear. It was such a savage depiction of the old pedant that Charles had felt ashamed to be amongst the laughing crowd. Reynie must have been there in his role as censor, Charles supposes, sat at the back in the darkness in judgement.

'Literature is a pit of vipers,' Reynie notes. 'Though the play did raise a few good points about the dangers of these so-called clever women, did it not? I am starting to wonder whether we have given them too many allowances on account of their sex, and so need to correct our path.'

Charles's sense of honour means he cannot let this pass, though he is wary of provoking this man. 'Much as I admire what you have achieved in Paris, Reynie, surely even you cannot police women's ability to think?'

'Haha! Perhaps that's true, though you know I love a challenge. But truly, when not applauding the humiliation of your fellow scribes, how are you filling your time? A man like yourself. You must be bored, out of the cut and thrust of the real action.' He gestures at the Latin books on the table. 'You are surely underused as a governess.'

'I love my sons dearly. Time spent with those you love is scarcely wasted,' Perrault says, deciding not to take the bait of offence. Although he has never quite cared for Reynie, he reminds himself that he does appreciate his efficiency: he certainly gets things done. Paris is surely the better for him as a whole, although it always strikes him that the man lacks a certain necessary compassion for those under his care – Reynie would simply sweep up the poor if he could, and dump them all in the Bastille. Still, Charles tells himself that he can withstand a little teasing.

'I hear you love to tell children's tales too, these days – the kind a wet nurse might read to a little girl?'

'Pardon me?' Perrault asks, trying to find his bearings. For this feels more than teasing; closer to a taunt. He becomes freshly conscious of having to choose his words with great delicacy. 'Ah! I mean, I suppose you are referring to the entertainment at the salons of Madame d'Aulnoy? If so, I will confess I have indulged in the frivolity once or twice, the tales the women tell are just – a delightful pastime, a frippery to while away a cup of drinking chocolate, nothing worthy of your grave attention, I'm sure.'

'A little fly said otherwise,' Reynie replies, tilting his head very calmly, moistening his cushiony mouth. Slowing down to enjoy himself. 'It landed on some horse dung on the Pont Neuf, you see, making all this buzzing racket, and when I leant in a little closer I heard them say something about princesses having bastards. Monstrous queens. Bzzzzzzt bzzzt. That kind of thing.'

'You know the tales yourself, though, from childhood surely?' Perrault says quietly, whilst mentally scanning the room from the other night's salon, to think who might be in the chief of police's pay. The story Reynie references is his cousin's, perhaps, or his own with which he followed it – the tale of 'The Sleeping Beauty in the Woods'. He had been pleased with it, particularly the passage where a deep sleep fell over the housekeepers, the chambermaids, the court officials, the cooks, the pageboys, the stable boys, the Swiss guards, and even the princess's little lapdog Puff (a lovely touch!). But perhaps he got carried away with himself in the second half, when Sleeping Beauty went back to the prince's house only to find out that his mother was part-ogre, and wanted to eat her small children in delicious sauces.

Anyway, the evil queen was definitely not Athénaïs, or maybe only a tiny bit.

There were several new people at the salon, though: the Duchess of Nemours; Henriette's cousin. Marie must be more careful who she lets into her home. He must be more careful what he says in her home. Perrault feels his chest tighten a little, when he thinks of people muttering slurs about Marie's salons; trying to sully them with inference. 'You need not pay some spy, Reynie, to repeat to you the story of "The Sleeping Beauty in the Woods" when you surely heard it yourself as a babe-in-arms. Even the king himself enjoyed such tales as a boy. You cannot search for the politic in tales as old as time.'

'But why tell them in rooms from which children are absent? Why now, during the reign of His Majesty Louis XIV?'

Except Marie d'Aulnoy has been a spy – the thought jumps into Perrault's brain like a louse, proceeds to suck and itch. Surely Marie is not in Reynie's pay, though? Surely she is not surveilling her own friends? No, he is vile to even think of it, he will not – her salon is not some kind of honeytrap. She is not Reynie's shitty little 'fly'! But still the thought pulses, tics, and he must swat it off in shame. 'You know it has been a hard winter,' Charles says instead, reaching for the easiest truth to hand. 'It is unsurprising escapism is in fashion, my friend. But surely you did not come here to discuss such scraps of fluff? Ladies daydreaming of princes in their private rooms? Do me the obligation of telling me your real intent. These insinuations are surely meant only as a little light pressure.'

'Ha! You understand, Perrault. Very well then, let's talk of grown men's subjects. You've heard rumours, I'm sure, around what they are calling the Affair of the Poisons?'

'Of course.'

'Well things have gained a certain momentum. Last week I arrested La Voisin.'

'Good God,' Perrault says, for he knows what this means.

'Quite,' Reynie says. 'She is di-a-bolical.' The 'she' in this is quite ambiguous, Perrault thinks. Athénaïs. Has Reynie really declared war upon the king's official mistress?

'Understandably, the king has become very vexed by this loose talk of poisoners. All of Versailles is in a panic about inheritance powders, so much so that hardly anyone has been enjoying their food, so I was given the dispensation to root out all those who sell such things, all the poisoners of Paris. Well, you can imagine, I was elated to do this, Perrault. I hate such people: so-called fortune tellers, alchemists, midwives, astrologers, magicians, chiromancers. All of their scrubby little premises; seances and abortions on the same rickety bloodstained tables; mixing up their fake aphrodisiacs out of feathers and crocodile eggs. I'm more than glad to cleanse this city of the whole damn lot. I had the least of them whipped, others tortured.

'Soon I felt I'd nearly fulfilled my duty to eradicate the

canker – well, all but one source. For I'd been told to steer clear of the midwife La Voisin, even after that poisoner Madame Bosse fingered her for selling powders. Even though she's known as the "duchess amongst witches" – so many well-connected women seek out her society, you see, she almost seems respectable. She holds parties in her gardens, with violins, where she reads fortunes in faces and palms, as if it is a party-game! But my curiosity got the better of me, so one night I sought her out.

'I found her in that tatty red robe with the eagle on it; stinking drunk. Her whole place so decadent – everywhere expensive trinkets, vases, statues, but everything dusty or grimy; mirrors you could barely see your face in; the hems of her velvet curtains stained with blood. And I could see, on her shelves, so many powders: I asked if they were poisons but she slurred out no, they were love potions. The bones of toads, snakeskin, the teeth of moles, Spanish fly, iron filings, human blood and mummy. Oh, maybe some human remains, the ashes of a foetus for example. Love potions! It sickens me what horrors women will partake in, under the name of romantic love. It is not love at all, but lust that drives them, that rancid lust for possession! I must admit that her head was slumping, so I roused her with a flame held against her palm. I wonder if La Voisin saw her future there, in the singeing flesh? Oh, she confessed to her black masses then: a baby held above a bowl; its throat slit and poured. A woman's naked body the very altar. Athénaïs's naked body.'

Perrault lets out a horrible moan. 'I don't want to hear

this, Reynie,' he says. 'I do not wish to be your confidant in this. I very much wish I could unhear it.'

'Her yard is full of bones. It is a charnel house. Athenaïs wanted a love potion to keep the king's favour, so they prayed to the devil. They mashed up babies' bones and blood, and slipped the foul mixture into our king's food, Perrault. For years! *Years.* I will not have her in this city. I am establishing a chambre ardente and that is that.' His big fist closes on itself.

'A burning court?'

'We must burn the witch. All the witches.'

'And why do you come to me?' Perrault asks. 'Why do you disturb me here?'

'You know that Athenaïs is the reason why you lost your position at Versailles. She is your enemy, Perrault. Assist me in getting rid of her, and you'll be invited back to the court by Madame de Maintenon, you have her word. This new mistress, Maintenon, is a good religious woman; God-fearing. She wants this plague gone from France as much as we do.'

'But I do not—'

'Do you not suspect that Athenaïs killed your old companion, Colbert? That she poisoned him, despite his loyalty, simply to be sure? Were you not there when she brought in that petition for the king that we now believe to have been dipped in poison – which God in his infinite wisdom made him too busy that day to pick up, and which further disappeared? It was you who told me that petition had vanished. You must testify against her, Perrault.'

139

'No,' Perrault says, shaking his head. 'Do you not know what Colbert used to say to me? *Testis linus, testis nullas.* One accusation means none. No no, Reynie, you mistake me for someone else, for I do not know anything of poison. Suspicion and speculation are not evidence. I am not so shrewd as you. I am no hero in a story who can trick the witch into the pot of boiling oil. I'm just a tired man who wants to stay at home with my books and my sons.'

'Very well,' Reynie says, standing up and blinking slowly. 'Very well, Charles, as you wish. If you do not want to help your friends, so be it.'

Which friends? Charles thinks helplessly, as Reynie exits his house. *Which friends does he mean?*

Afterwards, as Charles goes up to bed, he pauses at the door of his wife's old room. He has not touched anything inside: her brushes and mirror are still laid out on the dressing table. He does not open the door, which he always keeps locked, but rests his forehead against it. He likes to pretend that she is just behind the door, doing the same, and they are almost touching. 'I love you,' he murmurs aloud.

His marriage was a love-match, that rare thing. His family told him her dowry was not big enough, but he defied them. All his ambitions fell away, when he was in a room with her: he wanted nothing more than her wise face, her clear eyes. But she died in there. He will never forgive himself. He was at Versailles that day, finalizing some petty architectural plan for Athénaïs – a little pleasure-house decorated with white and blue delft tiles – when the baby came out very fast, a week early, and then her sickness came on too, so quickly, something galloping through her blood. The doctor bled her; the doctor bled his dying wife before Perrault could get back and stop him. Some useless bullshitting bastard in his black cloak, finishing her off; making sure.

The horror of death is that it separates you from those you love forever, that is the truth: if you feel no love in your heart, like Reynie, then death must seem a paltry thing. Perrault used to pray to God at night, but now it makes him feel a fool. It's so performative. For there is no God who can see into every skull – God is not the chief of police; his ranks of angels are not 'flies' surveilling our every word and deed. Now he talks to his wife in his house instead, although he knows she cannot hear him either. Nobody can hear him. It's so obvious: the abyss. *I'm so, so sorry. I don't know what to do. Everything's a mess since you left.* Crying makes him feel a fool, but he is weeping now, unstoppably. It's so performative. Who does he do this all for? Oh, what is the meaning?

(He does not know about us yet, of course, reader. And though I'm no angel, I must say I have been mistaken for one, my feathers being so lovely and white.)

15. The Tale of Bluebeard

Once upon a time, there lived a hugely wealthy man who owned grand houses in both the town and country, stuffed with silver and gold cutlery, silk dressing gowns, and furniture inlaid with ebony and mother-of-pearl. He even owned a gilded carriage! But he lacked the one possession that he coveted most, which was a wife. For, you see, he had a long blue beard that made him look so grotesque, all the girls turned their faces away from him.

Now, it happened this Bluebeard had a new neighbour, a widow with two grown sons and two grown daughters. One day, Bluebeard asked for one of the daughters in marriage – telling the widow that, in truth, he didn't mind which – and the widow, who was always very worried about money, saw this as an opportunity to enrich the family. Unfortunately for her, when she told her daughters of the offer there was much squabbling in the household over what to do, for neither daughter fancied marrying a bluebearded man, whilst they had also heard some off-putting rumours in the town – there were people who insisted that Bluebeard had married several wives before, and no one seemed able to say what had happened to them.

Deciding to charm them, Bluebeard invited the mother, the daughters and three of their best friends to his country manor for a week. They accepted and had, it must be said, a fabulous time, for there were parties, dances, feasts, hunts and card games. All night they stayed up playing pranks or quaffing champagne, and nobody went to bed. The youngest daughter even began to think that her neighbour's beard wasn't *that* blue, it only had a faint sheen, as on a plump blue-bottle's abdomen. When they returned home, she agreed to the marriage.

A month later, Bluebeard told his wife that he was going on an important business trip. 'Send for your friends and family,' he said. 'Amuse yourselves! Here are the keys: this opens my safe; this my casket of jewels; this is the master-key to all my apartments. I only ask one thing – do you see this little key, darling wife? It opens the room at the end of the great gallery. That little room is forbidden, I'm afraid. And I warn you, if you open it, I won't be able to control my anger.'

Once she had promised to obey his instructions, Blue-beard left on his journey. His wife's good friends were there in minutes, impatient to see the riches of their friend's new house (but still slightly nervous of her husband because of his blue beard). They poked through all the luxurious rooms, closets and wardrobes; admired the tapestry, beds, couches, cabinets, stands, tables and magnificent silver-framed look-ing glasses, in which you could see yourself from head to toe.

But the new bride felt a growing impatience to open that little room by the great gallery. It seemed to beckon. What might it contain? Her curiosity was so consuming that, with-out considering how rude it was to leave her guests, she hurried down a back staircase, so hastily that she nearly broke her neck twice (or some say thrice). At the door, she paused for a while, thinking of her promise, and also considering

143

how Bluebeard might punish her if she was disobedient, but the temptation was too strong. Taking the little key, aquiver with fear and anticipation, she opened the door.

At first it was hard to see, because the windows were shut. After some moments, as her eyes adjusted to the gloom, she began to perceive that several women seemed to be hung on the walls, as if on meat-hooks. Face to the wall. Their limbs had the pallor of death about them, and the floor was slippery with their blood. The room stank of rotting meat; a fly landed on her nape. These were the wives, she realized. Bluebeard's other, vanished wives.

Thinking she would die of fear, the key jittered out of her hand.

Pulling herself together, she scrambled on the slippery floor for the key, locked the door again, and ran upstairs into her chamber, but there was no rest. The closet key was stained. She tried two or three times to wipe it, but the blood would not come out. In vain she washed and washed it, scrubbing it with soap and sand, but the key was a magic key, so she could never make it quite clean. When the stain was gone from one side, it reappeared again on the other, like a dark red shadow.

When Bluebeard returned from his journey the next morning, his bride tried to feign delight at his early homecoming. He asked her for the keys, which she gave him with such a wobbling hand that he immediately guessed what had happened. 'Where's the little closet key, my wife?' he asked.

'I must have left it upstairs on the table,' she said, swallowing. He made her fetch it.

'How come this key's so stained?'

144

'I don't know,' she said, her head dipping ready for a blow. Pale as a corpse.

'You don't know, wife?' replied Bluebeard. 'Well, *I* know. You wanted to look in the little room? Go and look, then – feast your eyes! It will be the last thing you see in this life. I'll hang you up in there with my other brides.' She threw herself weeping at her husband's feet then, begging for his mercy – it might have melted a rock, such was her beauty and sorrow, but Bluebeard's heart was harder than any rock. 'You must die,' he said, softly, stroking her hair. 'I'm sorry, darling, but you took me as your master. It's just the rule.'

'My family will miss me,' she said.

'Oh, people soon forget a girl.'

'Give me time to say my prayers, at least,' she begged, eyes iridescent with tears.

'A quarter of an hour,' said Bluebeard, not wishing to rush his enjoyment of this murder.

But her sister, Anne, was still in the house. Madame Bluebeard hissed down the corridor: 'Anne, are you there? Go up to the top of the tower to see if our brothers are coming; they promised they would visit today.' Anne consented and ran to the top of the tower. 'Sister Anne, do you see anyone coming?'

'Nothing but the sun, which makes a dust.'

Meanwhile Bluebeard, holding a great cutlass in his hand, cried to his bride as loud as he could: 'Time's up, wife, come down or I'll come up to you.'

'One moment longer,' she said, and then she hissed again: 'Anne, do you see anybody coming?'

'I see a great cloud of dust, which comes from this side.'

'Our brothers?'

'Sorry, sister, just a flock of sheep.'

'Come down!' ordered Bluebeard.

'One moment longer,' said his bride. 'Anne, do you see anybody coming?'

'I see,' she said, 'two horsemen, I think – but a great way off.'

'Our brothers! Oh, thank God! Give them a sign to make haste!'

Then Bluebeard roared so loudly the whole house shook. In distress Madame Bluebeard came down and threw herself at his feet, wailing, her hair fallen about her shoulders.

'Enough!' said Bluebeard. 'This is tiresome, darling. You must die now as the others did.' Then, taking hold of her hair with one hand, he lifted up his cutlass in the air with the other, about to chop off her head. The poor lady, squirming, pleaded for one more little moment of life.

'Commend yourself to God,' he said, lifting up his weapon, and—

A loud knocking at the gate stayed Bluebeard's hand. Then the gate burst open, and two horsemen ran towards Bluebeard, swords raised. Bluebeard tried to flee, stumbling, but the two brothers pursued him, plunging their swords through his body so that he fell with a terrible scream. It turned out that his blood was red like everyone else's.

It was a strange fact that though he had married many wives, Bluebeard had produced no heirs. His wife inherited all of his estate. She gave some of the wealth to her brothers and sister, and used the rest to marry a worthy gentleman, who made her forget the sorry days she spent with Bluebeard.

A moral:

If you are curious, regret
May be the only prize you get.
Sometimes in life we must believe
(Pandora taught us this, and Eve).
It's not always our place to know.
Such satisfaction comes then goes —
A fleet sensation that can kill,
Or leave a most expensive bill.

Another moral:

No modern husband would now dare
To have a locked and bloody lair —
And if his beard is peacock blue
He still does what he's told to do.

16. The Tale of Persinette

In Paris, shivering with sweat, Charles Perrault wakes from a nightmare and goes straight to his desk by the small window to light a candle. It is just past one. Within a couple of hours, in a fever, 'Barbe Bleue' has poured out of him – it seems something other than himself; some toxin puked up; a darkness loosed from his bowels by an emetic.

Since then, there has, of course, been much speculation about the inspiration for this peculiar and haunting story. Years afterwards people will exchange many theories – there are some, in France, who say it must be inspired by the fifteenth-century serial killer Gilles de Rais, who murdered many children for occult purposes, pampering and drugging them, then stripping the children naked and hanging them with ropes from a hook. Given what Reynie has told Perrault of the witch La Voisin, has this long-ago story somehow been stirred up, a foul sediment in his soul?

If so, though, Perrault does not make this connection himself. In fact, he does not understand his story at all, as the two rhyming morals reveal. Although he labours over these most of all, neither is quite right. For the girl is rewarded and not punished, in the end, for her curiosity. And modern women aren't the masters of their husbands either – good God, what a glib conclusion that is! He imagines it will make them laugh at the salon, but not Madame d'Aulnoy, whose own Barbe Bleue still lurks somewhere offstage. Still, the tale has the merit of containing no kings or queens at least. Unable to see what lurks in the depths of his own text, he decides to take it with him to the salon in the evening. Perhaps all storytellers have been known to expose themselves so.

Morning comes, beautifully sunny, as if night itself was just a bad dream. Paris looks lovely, the Seine glittering like a sardine; all the markets of Les Halles with their stalls loaded with parsley, asparagus, artichokes, hare, roses, fresh bread, chestnuts, pale soft cheeses. Even the beggars almost picturesque, part of the teeming life. Flurries of sparrows. Ladies twirling their parasols outside the Saint-Sulpice like wands.

Perrault falls upon his breakfast – bread dipped in wine – ravenously, running on adrenalin now. 'Please procure me a blue beard,' he tells his slightly baffled servants, without further explanation.

After helping his sons with their rhetoric, he sets out into the city to make some calls – his brother's house, a tailor – stopping at a bookseller to purchase a book for Marie, too. A token to let her know how he appreciates the salons, the small shining spot in his life they have been this last year. It is something he feels all the more keenly, now he has the sickly sensation that they might be under threat. It is a very fine edition of the recent novel *La Princesse de Clèves* by Anon (a woman, he thinks, and he should very much like to have Marie's own insight into this), that feels new in its realism and psychological insight. He hopes to please her.

Afterwards he comes home and somehow falls into a fitful, sordid nap on his bed, then wakes up groggy and hard; fully clothed; a blue beard making a gigantic, pallid face of the pillow beside him. 'Ugh!' he gasps. Is he awake? But yes – it is an offcut of fur, stroked against the grain, its mouth a knife-slash. It has been daubed with blue paint; secured with a blue ribbon. It is his dream come true. As the clock says six, Perrault leaps to his feet, splashes his face with cold water and calls for the carriage.

When the salon gathers, Briou is noticeably not there, although Charlotte-Rose is, her jaw lightly clenched with defiance, a new determination detectable in her step. No one mentions the annulled marriage, although they have all of course heard of it by now.

The abbé seems very quiet and suppressed, simmering with anger. The morning papers implied that Molière's new play has the whole of Paris laughing at his poems, but he is not yet sure how bad the damage is. He cannot go to watch *The Clever Women*, and have the whole audience turn to gape at him! Perhaps he should go incognito. But no, instead he is unable to stop imagining the play in his mind, which is in many ways worse: inventing every wounding word; each wittily rhymed jab. That title even, *The Clever Women* – perhaps it is associating with this very salon that has brought such disrepute upon his shoulders! He has been too benevolent in coming here – his sincere wish to entertain and educate these women has been twisted and turned against him. And were these salonnières there too, in the audience for this play, betraying him with their titters and applause? The drapes beneath his eyes hang like moth-eaten theatre curtains, about to open on the final act of some tragedy.

Madame de Murat arrives, peeling off her red riding hood and accepting a lemon sherbet. Some other faces float in, that Perrault does not recognize. The Princesse de Conti lights her pipe with a hand that betrays emotion, her nostrils flaring as she exhales. The letter has not resurfaced, and she is trying not to worry about where it is now – she is amongst friends at the salon and is their patron even, in some cases, whilst her father's name is great protection. Surely it has just ended up in some crack; behind some cabinet? Still, she has not written again, but has resolved this time to speak to Henriette directly – to corner her, somehow, even for just a moment, and make her understand how ardently she is admired. 'Henriette,' she says. 'What a pleasure. I hope we shall have another of your tales tonight? I have yearned for your bracing wit these last weeks.'

'Then I will attempt to sate that yearning,' Henriette replies, smiling at the princess, but then looking down briskly, away from those brooding eyes.

'For you,' Charles tells Marie, when he gets a moment, handing her the gift, which she unwraps. 'Just a trifle. Perhaps you have it already. Perhaps you *are* Anon, and I am making a fool of myself! But I could not help thinking, as I read it, how much I desired to discuss the book with you and hear your thoughts on it.' Charles has a knack, she realizes, for looking at you very directly as he speaks, as if you were the only person in the room, his laugh-lines crinkling warmly. It crosses her mind that his wife must have thought herself lucky. Perhaps he is looking for a new wife – men of his standing usually are – but Marie tells herself he can't be flirting with her. She is still married to the baron in the eyes of the law, and, even if she were not, Charles is sure to want a younger bride, not damaged goods such as herself – his gesture seems, instead, touchingly platonic.

'Thank you, Charles,' Marie replies, with a smile that makes him feel gently illumined by her favour. 'You are a generous friend. I don't yet have a copy and have heard much chat about it. That is very kind, we shall discuss it at length!'

'I sincerely hope so.'

'Now, we have coffee with milk for those who wish to try a cup!' Madame d'Aulnoy announces to the room. And then: 'It looks quite murky, but it is the new fashion according to *Le Mercure galant*. Charles, would you mind awfully starting the tales for us tonight? Some of the others are running late.'

'I'd be honoured, Marie,' Perrault tells her, taking a hesitant sip of the bitter, muddy brew.

Angélique is recruited to play the young bride – which seems to delight her, as she gets to wear the wedding frock from the fancy-dress chest: 'The more times the better, don't you think?' she jokes – whilst Perrault himself sports the grotesque blue beard and waves around a cutlass. But he is nervous. The undertow of anxiety is still in his bloodstream, and is now mingling with the caffeine. He ought to have passed on some kind of warning to Marie, then, when he had the chance to talk to her directly – oughtn't he? Except what if she's the fly? Except what if she isn't? Except what if the women here are truly in danger of being exiled, like that acting troupe, or sent to some godawful convent miles from Paris?

He finds himself putting on a rather ill-advised Eastern accent. He is shaking slightly. Despite this, they laugh from the start, and the tale goes well. There is a true gasp of shock when the contents of the little room are revealed, and, when Bluebeard is slain, substantial applause. The rhyming morals, though, don't quite land – Perrault knows this. As the room expects such poetic flourishes from him now, he offers both up, but with an apologetic shrug. 'Which do you think is better? I only wrote them last night, and I am not sure I've quite got the moral right yet, I must confess.'

'Well the second one's just a cheap and nasty lie and you know it,' Henriette snaps straight away, her voice too quick with agitation. 'Is it nags you think us all, Perrault? Or whores perhaps? Or fishwives?'

'Yes,' he says, accepting the blow. 'I did think maybe not that one. You are right. Although I imagine you, Henriette, are quite the Amazon at home!' It is a terrible joke. He realizes this immediately. Didn't he notice, at church, at the theatre, how she visibly shrinks in her husband's presence? Has the coffee made his eyelid start to twitch?

'Just because I have committed some sins does not mean I commit them all,' Henriette replies (quoting Athénaïs), her smile as bitter as the dregs in his cup.

'I always think it strange,' Madame d'Aulnoy says – rather coolly, now he has upset her friend, for they stick together these women – 'when a fine writer condemns curiosity too. Is it not what fuels our pen?'

'But we must remember Eve, madame,' he replies. (Eve! Why is he dragging up that worn-out woman again in this company? How lazy his so-called wit, that can only think of Eve!)

'Yet I must admit I have never *quite* understood the moral of that tale either, however many patient priests try to explain it to me,' Marie replies, carefully, for she is surely treading dangerously – the abbé already puffing up a little as she speaks. 'It seems to be that we should believe what we're told, is that right, Charles? And do you always believe what you're told? Or is that rule just for women?'

'I'm – I suppose it all depends on the context, doesn't it,' Perrault replies, sadly backing into his corner, trying to discern her intent. 'And precisely who is telling.'

'Well, it is the Bible, I believe, that says all women are cursed – that we must suffer agonies in childbirth, for the sake of one woman's curiosity.' Charles feels out of his depth then. He cannot fathom her depths; he has swum out into them too far. Why is she touching on this tender subject, when she knows what happened to his wife? Her brown eyes suddenly don't seem kind, but disturbingly calm and emotionless. Yet, to know there is this vast, alert intelligence whirring behind them! That other thought, again: what if she will report everything he says here back to Reynie? He swats it down, he swats it down.

'I can assure you I always believe the Bible,' he blusters, a hint of anger in his voice. 'Any problems with interpretation must lie within our flawed understanding, seeing as we do through a glass darkly, as the Apostle Paul famously explains.'

'*The eye is not satisfied with seeing*,' intones the abbé, bitterly. 'Ecclesiastes 1:8. My own translation from the original Hebrew, of course. Curiosity only torments, it cannot sate! Perrault has done well to remember he's a Christian when penning that moral; I must say it makes a change in these decadent circles.'

'So I presume your grandmother didn't teach you this one?' Henriette asks Charles, always keen to change the subject from religion. 'I can hardly picture you, sire, as an adorable little baby suck-a-thumb, your grandmother beginning: "Once upon a time there was a mass murderer . . ."'

'Is it even a fairy tale, technically?' Charlotte-Rose asks, hesitantly, not sure if she ought to draw attention to herself. But she has been working on her first conte de fées all day, grappling with such questions of craft, and is genuinely unsure.

'There's a magic key!' Télésille cries out, always a student with the correct answer. 'That's the magical element, isn't it, cousin?'

'Yes, about that,' Henriette shoots back, sharp as ever.

'Isn't that rather excessive? It occurs to me that the tale might easily be a metaphor for childbirth, actually, with the virgin bride's understandable fear of the wedding bed. Her husband's bloody key is, well – it's very difficult not to interpret that image rather crudely. All the other wives who've died because he opened their locks.'

Perrault feels everything running away from him then, blurring. A naked feeling. Needing to sit down, suddenly, he tears off his blue beard and slumps on the sofa, saddened and injured. 'I understand your concerns, ladies! It is a first draft, and I clearly have much work to do. I have taken on board your comments and shall work upon my morals.'

'Oh, don't listen – I think this tale will be all the rage,' Angélique tells him, bounteous in her praise. Having taken off the wedding dress, she is now adjusting her spilling bosom and smoothing her wig with her fingers, before taking a sip of milky coffee with three sugars. 'I think you've written a hit, Charles, I do! It's so creepy! And so satisfying at the conclusion, isn't it, the way the man gets stabbed to death and she keeps all his money?' Angélique has had a bad week, but this hopeful narrative has given her a little fillip.

After refreshments, the next performer will be Charlotte-Rose de La Force. It is on this occasion she debuts her story 'Persinette', which will later be published in her 1698 book *Les Contes des Contes*, and gain her fame as an early version of that tale you might know as 'Rapunzel'. This evening she is on remarkably good form, despite her awareness of whispers. There is something about the whole squalid little episode with Briou that, for all the social embarrassment she feels, she has still found strangely renewing – at first, you see, she thought she was heartbroken, but then she realized that she wasn't, and now Charlotte-Rose feels almost gratified by her own impulsive foolishness. The gossip will turn at last, she hopes, into a kind of legend. She has won a secret history of her own; experience; adventures of which to tell.

And, knowing now that a prince is never going to rescue her from her dreary life as lady-in-waiting – that such hope was always just a castle in the air – she has made a decision, deep inside her heart, that she must rescue herself by the pen. Why should she renounce romance, for which she has such aptitude? Or, that is, she will renounce it only in real life, but not on the page.

Charlotte-Rose asks Henriette to be Persinette. 'Oh, perhaps I'm a little ironical for such a role, dear Charlotte-Rose,' she replies.

'But this is a princess who is perfectly bored! There is a long wig with plaits, put that on please! Oh, it suits you.' Madame Miaou springs then from Angélique's arms and tries to snatch the end of the plait, leaping up with her little claws aloft as for a golden bird. 'We have our bad fairy, it seems,' Charlotte-Rose notes, 'but we seem to have mislaid our Prince Charming on this occasion.' This self-deprecating humour raises a great chuckle from the crowd, who feel appeased and reassured by such an acknowledgement of recent events.

'Perhaps Abbé Cotin,' Télésille suggests, well meaning,

for he is not really anyone's idea of a prince, even hers, but she witnessed Molière's latest play the other night, and felt it amounted to bullying (it has not yet occurred to her that perhaps she, too, is the subject of the play-wright's satire. How rare it is, reader, that audiences recognize themselves!).

Truth be told, Télésille could not resist writing a dozen long letters summarizing the major plot-points upon her return home, but still, she is trying to bolster the poor unfortunate abbé now. 'Although,' she adds, beset by sudden doubts, 'is the role quite suitable for an abbé, Charlotte-Rose?'

Henriette remembers with a shudder how last time she and the abbé were acting out a tale, he put his moist little hand on her knee. 'Is it the prince bit you're wor-ried about?' she asks, sourly. 'Or the charm?'

'I shall play the prince,' the Princesse de Conti's voice comes, recognizing that Henriette needs her assistance. She gulps her glass of red wine. She has lost weight. Her cheeks are slightly sunken, so the cheekbones stand out.

'Ah, wonderful!' Charlotte-Rose replies, delighted, for Her Highness so rarely gets involved. 'I am grateful, princess. You will make a very dashing substitute.' She hardly notices Henriette's body tense up. So it is that, summoning all her nerve for this debut, stepping into the room's centre – that pool of attention – Charlotte-Rose stands up tall, holds in her stomach from habit, and begins: 'Once upon a time . . .'

Now, this tale begins with a couple awaiting the birth of their first child. They live next door to a fairy whose walled garden is filled with vegetables and herbs, including parsley, which the pregnant wife desperately craves. When the husband slips through the gate to steal some and is caught, the fairy responds by saying that he may take it, but he will owe her the child.

Once she is born, the fairy treasures the girl-child, who she christens Persinette (meaning 'little parsley'. Rapunzel, in later versions, is a reference to rampion: a bitter green, spinachy plant). It is only when Persinette is twelve years old that the fairy – worried about male attention – locks the girl in a silver tower in the forest.

Persinette is not denied any luxury: all the dresses, muffs and fans that a girl might dream of are hers; there is fine food to eat. But she soon finds everything lonely and dull. Her only company is an occasional visit from the fairy, who cries out, 'Persinette, Persinette, let down your hair,' and clambers up her shimmering, golden, thirty-eight-yard plaits.

Things change one day when a hunting prince hears Persinette singing, and falls in love with her voice. Behind a tree, listening in, he hears the fairy telling Persinette to lower her hair. That night he imitates the fairy's voice, and clambers up himself.

(The princess acts this out now, making her way up the wig towards Henriette, hand over hand, her gaze very level and deep and languishing. Henriette can hardly stand it, with all these other eyes upon them.)

The prince woos her. Persinette becomes pregnant.

(The Princesse de Conti hands Henriette a cushion for this, which she stuffs up the front of her mantua, to much amusement. Even Henriette's face breaks a little with the relief of levity.)

Seeing the bump, the fairy – livid – forces Persinette to confess the truth. As punishment, the fairy snips off Persinette's braids, then carries her far away (by cloud) to a hut on a seashore, where there is a magical food supply. There, Persinette will give birth to twins.

Meanwhile, the evil fairy lures the prince up the tower by mimicking Persinette's song – for she is quite the mockingbird – and lowering one of the girl's braids as a rope. At the top, she tells him the princess is no longer his; hurls him back down, so he tumbles into sharp thorns which pierce his eyes and blind him. The lovelorn prince spends a year wandering the wilderness, crying out: *Persinette, my darling! My Persinette, where are you?*

(The Princesse de Conti makes a good job of stumbling round blind, the wine adding to the verity perhaps, and trips over Angélique's foot, as if by accident, tumbling abject to the earth and pounding it, crying out: 'My love! My love!')

There is a lot of emotion in the room, suddenly, when everyone realizes that Persinette is going to rescue the prince, because there has been rumour of Charlotte-Rose attempting to break into a castle to free Briou after their ill-fated marriage – dressed as an ape, some say, or a bear, though it scarcely seems plausible.

Charlotte-Rose has to fight through her emotion too, because she herself is thinking – how could she not? – of how desperately grateful Briou was when she found him, in his bedchamber; his tender, pitiful moans as they made love on the fur; his sob of relief as he came, almost cowering. How she felt in that moment – as all rescuers must feel – as though his happiness was entirely in her power.

And then how somehow, as they slept, the thorns grew up around him. In the morning he was awake before she was, pacing and fidgety in a blade of daylight, filled by that dangerous, unfocused anger that looks for a place to land. He told her to leave; to get out of the castle before she was seen. 'How the fuck am I supposed to know how? This isn't my mess, Charlotte-Rose! Do you want me to be disinherited, is that what you want? If anyone asks, I haven't seen you, all right? All right?' And Briou looked at her then as if he already wasn't seeing her; as if he had stopped seeing her. *My make-up*, she'd thought, in a trembling panic. *I forgot to get up early and do my make-up.*

Their marriage has been declared void now. Briou's father knew what strings to pull, to have her written out of their family history. There is rumour Briou is back in Paris again already, incognito.

Don't think of him, she tells herself. *This is more important than him.* For in this fairy story, Charlotte-Rose's story, love is victorious. Persinette comes upon the prince one day in the woods. Her blinded beloved looks so pitiful that she takes his head into her lap and begins to weep, so the tears touch his eyelids, which spring open – eyes clear and grey and full of love. Healed by her love.

(It is really incredibly romantic. As the Princesse de Conti opens her eyes and looks up at Henriette, there are cheeks being dabbed around the room; guests virtually swooning. Unfortunately, Charlotte-Rose has not finished.)

'So, the family were reunited,' Charlotte-Rose concludes. 'But when they returned to the hut, the magic replenishing food had turned to stones, the water to poison, the herbs in the garden to toads and snakes, and the birds into harpies and enormous fire-breathing dragons with massive jaws which snatched up the baby twins, and they were about to die! Luckily the evil fairy turned up in a golden chariot, and let them live. The end.'

Perrault feels a small jolt of fear travel through him. Too many words he did not want to hear there: bad fairy, mockingbird, poisons, toads, snakes. Something about babies nearly being burned. But he claps, regardless: 'Bravo, bravo.'

'Oh, and the motto,' Charlotte-Rose adds, once the applause dies down. 'I thought I'd try out rhyme, in homage to you, Monsieur Perrault. Something like this.' And she reads out:

> *If you're a princess in a tower,*
> *More tired of life with every hour,*
> *Hoping he'll get you out of there,*
> *My main advice is grow your hair.*
> *Princes, for all they promise you,*
> *Turn out to need some saving too.*

'What a debut!' Marie d'Aulnoy says. 'Oh, Charlotte-Rose, you should be proud. It is a tale to be remembered! How marvellous that *she* saves *him*.'

'Although I think perhaps, madame, if you were hoping to publish, which you very much ought to consider for all our sakes,' Perrault says, hoping that flattery will encourage her to listen to this well-meant advice, 'perhaps you could end the tale a tad earlier? It would be much more touching to just finish with the tears, as they heal the prince's eyes: that scene is masterly.'

'I thought, at the end, perhaps I needed some magic to make it officially a fairy tale,' Charlotte-Rose admits. 'Cruel guardians, girls kept in towers, princes . . . I only wondered if it was all a bit too close to life and I needed to include some spells . . .'

'Well, yes,' says Télésille. 'Although –' she hesitates a moment '– is it all right if I give just the tiniest criticism too, as Charles did, and, well, because I was so very glad to have all your honest feedback on my own debut piece the other week? I just thought it was a little sad that Persinette had twins, because I felt she was a principled Christian girl so might defend her very honour and maidenhead with more alacrity than that. I mean, as my very close friend Mademoiselle de Scudéry says, of course, very famously: "The virtue which has never been attacked by temptation is deserving of no monument." So have her keep her virtue, and then at the end you could have a lovely church wedding which would be so romantic. But I'm old-fashioned in such notions, I know, and maybe all Parisians but me have decided such goings-on are quite au courant.'

'I have to say I agree with you,' the abbé tells Télésille, seizing his moment to press his moral superiority, the only card he knows for certain he has left. If they do not think him a prince then, fine, he will play the priest. Let them see who finds the judgement of Jesus Christ amusing! 'In fact, I would go further – it is time to get more church scenes altogether in these so-called fairy tales. If you wish to make them modern, why then you must excise their pagan roots and remember that we live in a Christian society! No fair virgin must ever obtain knowledge of a man, as it were, until explicitly permitted by our Lord and Master in Heaven. It is written in the Bible! You would have the wench damned like some pavement nymph!'

'But without the pregnancy there would be no risk of anyone finding out,' the Princesse de Conti says, exchanging a glance with Henriette. 'If they were careful.'

'Well make them have a secret wedding beforehand, then!' Télésille yelps, with the enthusiasm of someone who thinks they have just provided a fine, high-minded solution, rather than carelessly jabbed at an incredibly raw and recent wound. Charles puts his face in his hands with embarrassment.

Luckily Charlotte-Rose replies, 'Where do you get your ideas, Télésille? I'm sure I could never come up with such a notion!' allowing everyone to laugh again, with the reprieve.

'I loved it just as it was,' Marie says, and then, more softly, for Charlotte-Rose alone: 'You are an extraordinary writer and a brave one, my dear friend. The pen will give you your happy ending, I know it.' And Charlotte-Rose smiles back because she sort of knows it too.

Behind them, Henriette and the Princesse de Conti curtsey and sit down, the princess's hand touching the small of Henriette's back as they do. Madame de Murat's long eyes glittering; her body strung tight as a bow. Ah, these Modern Fairies! In each age-old tale they borrow there are hard-won truths, yet they overlook them again and again. Do they not realize that such a precise craving, as for parsley or bitter greens, can only ever be bartered for at the most terrible cost?

17. The Tale of the Rose

The hour after a salon is often Madame d'Aulnoy's favourite: that sense of completion. Berthe tidying up glasses with a cheerful tune; Mimi giving Judith's hair a hundred strokes of the brush by the fire; Thérèse keeping her watchful eye on the female greyhound, who has just given birth to a litter of squealing pups downstairs – who squirm and squidge like a basketful of blind mice – thus filling her middle daughter with a fierce protectiveness. Her youngest daughter Françoise and her pet, Belle-Belle – loosed from the contract of best behaviour – begin a raucous game of hide-and-seek around the house. Marie is ready to go upstairs with a cup of tea and her new book.

Not quite everyone has gone yet, though, for Angélique has asked to stay behind, desperate to talk of matters. So it is that the two women sit on the sofa a little while longer, Angélique sipping an apricot cordial that gives her mouth a sticky gleam; Marie taking another of the coffees with milk, which she imagines might be a necessary stimulant for these last minutes of a long evening.

'I've just had the most terrible couple of weeks, you won't believe,' Angélique is saying. 'I mean I've been very hurt by this whole business with Briou! You must have known about me and Briou, I mean, you're a woman of the world, Marie, you know how these things happen between a male and a female person. We just had a real understanding, I thought, it was just light between us – very playful – but for him to marry my friend – well, my friend's god-daughter – and he didn't even give me an inkling, I mean, not even a bit of time to prepare my reaction! Because my jaw dropped, I have to say, to the damn floor, when I heard – in a box at the opera, of all places – and it was so humiliating for me I had to virtually weep behind my fan. Luckily it was the tragedy of *Alceste*, if it had been a comedy it could have been much more embarrassing. I mean, did he not even think of my feelings? And what am I to say to Charlotte-Rose's godmother, when I was supposed to be keeping an eye on her? Although she was bearing up tonight, wasn't she? Perhaps it will be the making of Charlotte-Rose. And now the marriage is annulled I suppose it stings a little less. But anyway, Claude has threatened me with a lettre de cachet, again, on top of everything.'

'Oh, Angélique,' Marie says, shaking her head, for this part is serious. 'You must try and calm him down. Now the problem of Briou has been dealt with, perhaps you can attend to Claude's wounded pride a little, for your own sake?'

'Oh no no no,' Angélique says, shaking her head right back, far too gone now, in her addled self-absorption, to stoop to considering the private self of that villain, her husband. 'It's very far past that, Marie! He's gone far too far. And my valet Moura has been so understanding, you know, he's really surprisingly emotionally insightful for a valet, whilst he has his ambitions, of course, which I can help with – which I want to help with, for you know me, Marie, how generous I always am with my friends, for whom nothing's too much – it's a kind of fault really.'

'If you are planning something with Moura,' Marie says, apprehensively, 'I'm not sure that is prudent.'

'But she won, didn't she?'

'Who won?' Madame d'Aulnoy asks, unable to disguise a flash of exasperation at these private leaps that Angélique makes.

'The bride, in Charles's story. "Bluebeard". She really showed that swine, then ended up with everything, just as she deserved! And if she gave the brothers money afterwards, well what's wrong with that? Didn't they deserve some recognition for their service?'

'Please, stop thinking like this,' Madame d'Aulnoy tells Angélique, feeling the anxiety begin to seep in. 'This is real life. So many fairy tales have the logic of a dream – they seem to show action and consequence, but that's a trick. They reveal nothing but what the teller wishes to happen. Perrault wants Bluebeard dead, so he slaughtered him. Does Corneille not tell us: "An example is often a deceptive mirror"? In real life, I must assure you, the story does not end this way.'

But she has lost Angélique. 'I don't understand you,' her friend shrugs, suddenly ready for bed, having hoped for a little more support. She tickles Madame Miaou under her soft chin; rubs noses with her. 'I've never really enjoyed Corneille's plays, if I'm honest, they're so doomy-gloomy. Look. It is impossible for me to have any enjoyment of myself whilst my husband lives. And his health's too good for me to look for a quick revolution of fortune.'

'I am telling you I know how this story ends,' Marie says, her voice harder but hushed now, clearly not wanting the children to hear. 'Do not force me to remember what I do not care to. Please, I am trying to warn you for your own good.'

It is only then that Angélique realizes Marie is referring to her own plot against the baron – though that is hardly the same thing, she tells herself, given it was years ago and Marie was not, as far as she knows, under the shadow of any threat against her freedom when she framed her husband, and that whole plan of accusing the Baron d'Aulnoy of treason because he spoke against the king's taxes, from what she understands, was overcomplicated and not nearly as foolproof as a simple murder.

Still, Marie is getting a little testy – and the children are around, of course, which isn't ideal – so Angélique tells herself she must simply find another confidante who isn't cherishing a past trauma. It's disappointing, but luckily for Marie she is a generous friend. 'It's so late, I realize; I'm inconveniencing you, Marie.'

'You're not at all, Angélique, please.' Marie feels a sense of events slipping out of her control now, speeding towards some terrible end. 'I simply feel that, as a friend—'

'Well, Madame Miaou hasn't been aux toilettes, I

realize, and you know, Marie, how I always so admire your soft furnishings, so I think I'd better leave, don't you?'

Which is convenient for your storyteller, for whilst this is happening, a parallel narrative is also unfolding that we must follow closely. I wish to go and check in on Madame Henriette de Murat, who does not grasp that she is in grave danger as she walks up the steps to her front door.

The Princesse de Conti's carriage has dropped her here just moments ago, and it must be admitted that the effects of the journey are still visible on Henriette as she approaches her home: her sharp chin shines, the powder quite gone, and there is a small fair hair on her tongue; her knees are weak as a calf's; her wig is askew; she is outrageously happy.

'In vain I have struggled,' the princess whispered in her ear, that shivering breath sending every nerve in her body ringing, irresistible. 'Please do not trifle with me, Henriette.'

But the small step through Henriette's door, now, is from a comedy into a tragedy. Inside her hall, there is a wholly different temperature and tone of light, and her husband the Count de Murat stands there – simply stands there – as though he has been waiting like a hound for the hunt to begin.

You have perhaps, in some fairy tale or other, come across the conceit of the rose whose life seems the mirror of another's life? As a petal falls from the rose this person weakens, and, it is imagined, that when the final petal falls they will die. We may compare the count's love for Henriette to some such rose. There was a time when he was full of admiration for his witty, literate wife, well born and amusing, whose conversation was quite the toast of Paris, and the rose seemed quite perfect. But then, when a witticism of hers made him feel small, a petal fell. When they could not conceive – and the barrenness was surely hers, given her lack of maternal instinct and cultivated malevolence, not to mention the astringent douches she used in the past for a contraceptive method – another petal, another petal. When the count found a young mistress whose company was a comfort to him, all round soft edges and fond words: another petal. When he hit her for the first time, splitting her lip, but she did not beg his forgiveness and only curled it in that sarcastic manner of hers: another petal. And as the petals fell, Henriette found to her horror that her own life was wedded to this flower, and that as it diminished her own sense of self, too, seemed to diminish; her own heart to shrink in her chest. And at last, these recent months, she had taken to tiptoeing around the plant, barely daring to breathe near it for fear of disturbing that last petal, which will surely be the end of her.

Well, now she sees that petal tumble to the floor.

Rearing up, the count slams her against the wall to pin her by the neck, grunting only, 'BITCH, BITCH,' his hand a meat-hook from which Henriette dangles, chokes, making strangled airless noises as she kicks like a puppet. Both seem to shudder the same awful shudder, as if some powerful current fizzes and burns through them – snaps his neck back, makes her limbs jerk, presses his fingers in, further, tighter, as if their sole aim is to make a smaller cage.

Death is only a second away, surely, when Reynie steps into the hall, nonchalantly, stooping slightly so as not to bang his head on the frame. 'If I may request that you desist, count,' he says – as the hunter to his dog – 'I would much appreciate the courtesy.' The chief of police, you see, takes personal charge of every lettre de cachet, and he has come to deliver Henriette's.

'Apologies I wasn't here to welcome you personally, Madame de Murat,' he adds. 'Or may I call you Henriette? I think I will. I had to wash my hands. Perhaps your husband was telling you, in his manner, that I bring news of a dramatic change in your circumstances? Dear dear dear.'

'There was coarse language, sire, and a smattering of bestial grunts,' Henriette says, getting her breath and tongue back, 'if that is what you mean by his manner, though I personally thought it showed no manners at all.'

'You whore,' the count spits. 'You hear how she talks to me, Reynie?'

'I do, count, I do. I'm only sorry you've had to endure it so long. But never mind, I am here to ameliorate your condition. Henriette, Henriette, Henriette –' He shakes his head, terribly slowly. 'Your mother wishes you to know that she is disinheriting you, whilst I'm afraid you may find that there will be a forced hiatus in your literary career. As to your marriage, well – it seems in its death-throes. You see I have here' – he waves some papers in his big hand – 'a report accusing you of shocking practices and beliefs.'

'I've never been near La Voisin!' Madame de Murat cries out, knowing the rumours of the fortune teller's arrest and hoping that there has been some confusion. Yes, she did try to get pregnant, but not like that, only 'heating' her husband with spicy foods as was advised; she has never aborted a baby with wormwood or hyssop.

'Oh, I know that, madame, I know,' Reynie replies, the corner of his mouth twisting up. 'Believe me, I know who's been coming and going there. I'm talking about les-bi-an-ism. Unnatural relationships between women, as practised by that poet Sappho that les précieuses profess to love so well. You are being banished, Henriette de Murat. I have an order here from Louis XIV to lock you up in the Château de Loches, if I can persuade the count not to kill you first.'

'No,' she splutters. 'No! But I haven't—'

'Oh, but you have,' Reynie replies, 'you really have. And with his daughter it seems, though we don't mention that, but you'll understand the king does not approve of you perverting a member of the royal bloodline in this manner.' He shows that letter, then, written in the Princesse de Conti's hand, and how she scans through it – rapidly, thirstily, as if it is both poison and antidote:

... *Some say the day begins with God, but I began today, as every day, by thinking of the object of my love, for I think of her incessantly* . . .

. . . It is my destiny, I am sure of it, to weave my limbs with yours, to kiss you endlessly, everywhere, always.

My darling, I can think of nothing but that I am madly in love with you . . .

Oh, how Henriette weeps! For it is such an ill-fated, wild, unhinging thing, to both discover and lose – in the very same moment – your one true love.

18. The Tale of the Goose Girl

To make oeuf miroir, Anne taps the huge goose egg against the lip of the pan, so a series of tiny cracks appear in the white shell, like cracks of ice in a frozen lake, then she digs in her nails and pours the egg into the spitting fat.

Anne covers it with a lid for a minute. Her hands are red and thick from thirty years of cooking in various households, swollen-knuckled and scarred by metal trays and jumping oil and licks of flame – there is a touching courage about them. When she removes the lid, the very clear, viscous, sunlit albumen has turned white, whilst the large yellow yolk trembles sensuously beneath its faint crown, so golden as to tip into a parody of gold, with the wobble of a plump belly. Anne spoons over more fat. The edge catches a little rusty frizz. She slides the vast egg on to a plate.

Geese only lay rarely and mainly in summer. This morning a twelve-year-old goose girl with a lovely long pale throat and hair like corn – the kind a prince might easily fall in love with, if she did not smell of goose-shit – woke early, ready to herd her geese to the river, and, after they had jabbed and hissed at her – for they are not kindly charges – found the eggs, which she immediately gave to a farm-boy, who packed them in hay and rode them into market, where Anne bought them, thinking: goose eggs, what a treat.

Mimi looks happy, dipping her bread into the yolk of hers straight away so it gushes, a fountain of pure gold. They are all eating around the table: Mimi, Judith, Thérèse, Françoise, Berthe and Marie, who does not like airs and graces when there are no guests, but for all members of the household to eat together, with simple good food (though they have learnt to shut Belle-Belle upstairs at mealtimes). She is a decent employer, Anne has to admit, though a strange one who seems to keep many secrets – Thérèse and Françoise, for example, were both surely born long after Madame's break-up with the baron, who she's still married to in God's eyes, and they don't look a jot like their elder sister, Judith, but Anne supposes it's not for her to question the morals of her betters.

'Can we play spillikins?' Françoise asks, static-haired today, and always easily distracted. It is her latest favourite game, involving a teetering heap of small rods and a fearless hand.

'Finish your egg first,' Marie says. 'You've barely touched it. And use your knife and fork properly.'

'I'm *bored*.' Françoise performs the mime for bored, rolling her eyes, her whole little body a flounce.

'Don't be so rude, goose eggs are a treat.'

'Can monkeys eat them?'

'I'm going to pretend not to hear that.'

'You eat up your egg, mon chouchou,' Mimi tells the youngest daughter. 'It's full of goodness, an egg. It'll make you grow up big and strong as an Amazon. Was there any gossip at the market, then, Anne?'

'Well there was one nasty rumour,' Anne says, looking up at Marie to gauge her reaction, 'although probably it's nothing. But I did hear from another cook who lives across the road from her that the chief of police called at Madame de Murat's house last night.'

'Ooh, there's a thing!' Mimi says, unable to hide her interest at such high-quality hearsay.

Marie glances up from her egg, a horrible energy suddenly snapping her fully awake. She does not, in truth, like eggs that much; she finds them obscurely disturbing, like overripe fruit, and the goose egg is perhaps the eggiest egg of all. Last night, she did not sleep well, for Charles's story disturbed her – she knows she has a bloody chamber inside her soul that she must never enter, with those two dead babies inside it, and that beautiful young man, his head staring up at her from an executioner's basket – and Angélique's hints at plots hardly helped.

'But why would he call for Henriette?' Marie says, as though coming out of a daze. 'It must be the Count de Murat. He is – I don't think he is a terribly nice man.' She has noticed more than one bruise, and thick powder over a swollen eye, though when she has tried to speak to Henriette her friend has always dismissed it as a tiff. A normal domestic spat. *You know me, Marie, I do quite talk my way into these things.*

'It was Madame de Murat the chief of police left with, supposedly,' Anne says.

Of course, not knowing of Henriette and the princess's dalliance, Marie immediately thinks of Henriette's tales. Everyone knows that Reynie loves to censor, so is constantly banning books, and perhaps Henriette's stories have touched a nerve – the one called 'Young and Handsome', for example, about a king who stops loving his wife as she grows older and attaches himself to 'young beauties of the court' might have been rather on the nose; or 'The Palace of Revenge' (even the title of that), in which the castle is entirely lined with mirrors that induce violent passion, and at the end they are all smashed. Perhaps such a scene might be interpreted as a call to revolution – perhaps, to an extent, it *is* a call to revolution, sharp-tongued Madame de Murat hardly being known for a deep sense of satisfaction with things as they are.

But how could they have reached him, these tales, being only spoken as yet and not printed?

Charles Perrault knows Reynie, she realizes. He was a powerful man for many years, they must have had many dealings: the building of the Louvre by Charles's brother, at his commission; the opening of the Tuileries. But surely Charles would not betray them? She does not want to think that; these last months since he has started attending he has always seemed so – not humble, exactly, and he can definitely be slightly pompous, but, as she's come to know him, so warm and vulnerable and generous and complicated: such an entire person, somehow.

Oh, but what about his cousin, Télésille, whose ink is

so loose she cannot eat a macaroon without penning letters to half of Versailles about it? She would much rather suspect Télésille.

'Poor Henriette!' she cries. 'Oh, my friend! What can we do? We need to help her.' Her first impulse is to think that she must speak to Charles at once. But what if he's a spy? Then she notices something.

'Françoise, where is your egg?'

'In my tummy,' Françoise says, with her biggest liar's smile. She has two new teeth coming through before the older ones have fallen out: in a second row, like a shark. There is a scuffle of greyhound under the table. One emerges from beneath her chair with a glistening yellow nose.

'Maman,' red-haired Judith says, changing the subject in an attempt to protect her little sister, who she always finds adorable (or half-sister, of course, for she is old enough to appreciate that she looks different, and that the baron was no longer part of her mother's life when the stork delivered Thérèse and Françoise). 'Did the others tell you we got another invitation from the palace today, to another ball? Can we go again, as it was so pleasant last time? And this will be a summer one, in the gardens.' She smiles hopefully. 'I have been thinking that I should like a green dress, to complement my hair, if we might be able to afford new frocks.'

No one ever knows, in this house, really, if they are rich or poor, and where the money comes from – it seems Marie somehow magics it up. Perhaps she has some enchanted purse, a luxurious version of that porridge pot, that always has gold in it when you reach inside. The baron has cut them off financially, and wrote Madame d'Aulnoy and the girls out of his will years ago – though he is still alive out there somewhere, drinking himself to death: pissing the bed, falling asleep face down in his meals, yellowish, shaky, shrivelled to the size of a thumb.

'Is it a masked ball?' Françoise asks. 'I think I'd like to go as an elephant!' (She has a thing for elephants.)

'I'm sorry,' Marie says. 'I'm afraid not.'

'It's a shame it's not masked,' Thérèse says, shyly, as if she would prefer this too for other reasons, for she is always quick to obscure her timid, delicate face with her hair. 'Maybe we ought not to go, Mother, if you don't want us to.'

But Françoise has already opened the door to Belle-Belle, and is leading the monkey in a minuet. 'She's a good dancer for a monkey, isn't she, my ducks?' Mimi says. 'Do you think she'll turn out to be a monkey princess? Her nobility unrecognized, like in that story about the goose girl I used to tell you, with the talking horse's head on the wall?' It is another of Mimi's more brutal old favourites, with the false princess punished at the end: stripped naked and dragged over nails by two white horses until she is flayed to death.

See how Marie's brain whirs behind her gentle brown eyes, trying to play through a thousand games of consequences; think up viable excuses. How can one be so surrounded by love and yet be so horribly lonely? It all feels too much right now, with so little sleep, and with her dear friend Henriette being ridden, as they dance, into exile most probably. However, it is her deepest instinct to never ever let her daughters see even the slightest flash of panic cross her face, so it is to this first duty she attends.

19. The Tales of Ricdin-Ricdon and The Foolish Wishes

The Princesse de Conti stumbles through the space, woozily, late, wine-fuddled, somehow banging her shins or stubbing her toes on every single chair or table or pouffe stuffed with horsehair or leg or foot in the whole room, then drops the full weight of herself into the high-backed armchair. She lights her pipe with her face stuck in a kind of vicious, self-despising sneer.

It is a warm summer evening and many of the women hold fans that make a delicate breeze in the room. Angélique's new one depicts a sumptuous Venus emerging from a shell, surrounded by water-nymphs and chubby little putti. The air is sweet with lots of roses in vases – lemon and pink only, as Marie has a kind of superstitious feeling about white or red ones – whilst Anne has made some very good layered cake with puff pastry and frangipane, its combed glazing like marble tiles. 'Wine?' Marie offers her guests. Champagne does not feel right, being too celebratory, but she needs wine to get through tonight.

'Certainly,' Charles says softly. 'Wine would be very helpful. And may I help you serve, Marie?' It is the first salon since Henriette was arrested and there is an edge to the proceedings. The attendance is lighter than usual. Perhaps people are staying away? Charles feels slightly sickened by the thought he might be partially, obliquely responsible.

Though his pride might have been injured by the reception of his 'Bluebeard' at the last salon, Henriette's arrest at least persuades him that Madame d'Aulnoy is not likely to be Reynie's 'fly' – he has seen the tender friendship between the two when they speak together – and he is glad to be unburdened of that suspicion. But who is it if not her? The only regular who has never seemed truly part of the inner circle is Abbé Cotin, and that man has had reason to feel rejected by the literary set in recent months. But no, it cannot be the abbé – he is a man of God for goodness' sakes, however tedious and slandered. Charles wonders if he should have avoided the salon himself today, but he felt compelled to come – drawn back, as if by something unfinished.

'I thought, after Henriette's arrest, you might have cancelled the salon,' he tells Marie, quietly, under his breath lest the others should hear. 'I am very glad that you have not, but I feel we must tread carefully, in case – well, walls have ears in Paris. I just wanted you to know that I am entirely at your disposal.' His concern scares Marie a little: if Charles himself is taking the threat to her salon seriously, she is right to be anxious. Except she cannot help but take some comfort in it too – perhaps she needs help, to manage this situation, now Henriette is not beside her. She feels less alone as she nods her agreement.

'Thank you, Charles, that means a lot. Oh. Whatever is that smell?' she asks him. It is a strange goat's-wool smell, dirty – almost like a whiff of sulphur.

'Good God!' Charles cries and he bounds, like a wizard, across the room to where the Princesse de Conti's hair is on fire – she stumbled too close, it seems, to a candelabra – and hurls his Chablis over her.

'What the fuck?' she asks, with a kind of dead-eyed wonder.

'Apologies, Your Highness, your – your hair had caught light. The – the smell is of burning hair—'

The princess sniggers, weirdly. 'Thanks, Charles,' Marie says. 'BERTHE? Berthe, could you get the princess a handkerchief perhaps, to dry herself . . .' Oh God, thinks Marie, this isn't going to go well, at all. And Télésille is on first, who she has already tried and found guilty in the court of her mind, though she must attempt not to betray her suspicions too obviously.

Ever since the rumours swept through Paris that Henriette de Murat has been arrested for sexual depravity, Télésille – known to also belong to the inner circle of the Modern Fairies – has found herself barely able to keep up with the sheer volume of correspondence from both close and more distant friends enquiring after her privileged insights, to the extent that she has sprained her writing wrist. Still, she has laboured through the pain to finish her story, 'Ricdin-Ricdon', which perhaps you are familiar with as the earliest version of 'Rumpelstiltskin', and this time hopes that her upstanding moral message will not be muddled by her taste for retributive fictional violence.

'Would you like a glass of wine for your nerves, cousin?' Charles asks her.

'Oh no, I think I ought not to, until after my perform-ance. Wine always makes my tongue feel rather clumsy, not that it needs any help! Maybe a drinking chocolate, if there's any to hand? Though I'd hate to put anyone out, of course.'

'I'll ask Berthe, if I can catch her . . .'

Fifteen minutes later, chocolate finally procured, after Anne has found some cocoa and sugar in the kitchen and warmed the milk, and Berthe has brought it inside a delicate pink china cup, and Perrault has praised them all extravagantly, Télésille takes a sip, and gives a little sigh of appreciation, and begins her tale, inspired, she notes, by the gallant troubadours, and hopefully giving a fla-vour of Gaulish antiquity.

In this tale King Prudent is married to hard-working Queen Laborious, but their son is neither prudent nor hard-working and has a taste for balls and carousels, as well as games of tag and blind man's bluff, so earns the nickname Prince Lovejoy.

One day, separated from his companions whilst hunt-ing, Prince Lovejoy sees a beautiful girl being dragged roughly to a simple cottage by an ugly old crone. The girl wears a violet corset, has rustic hair, and holds a distaff and flax as if for spinning. When the prince questions the old woman's treatment of her daughter, she says, 'Have her, then, I'd gladly be rid of her. Daughters are such a burden. She's always spinning too, such a terrible bore.' So he lifts the young woman, who is called Rosanie, up on to his steed.

When the prince brings her home, Queen Laborious's

ears prick up at the mention of spinning, and she sets Rosanie to work on heaps of hemp from Syria, piles of flax from Flanders, and many other expensive fibres. But once alone the girl weeps and weeps, for she actually hates spinning, feels it as a torture, and can scarcely spin enough in a week to half-fill a spindle. Soon all the court are in love with this girl they call 'the Beautiful Spinner', but then the dread day comes when the queen wants to see her work.

Rosanie goes weeping into the gardens. As soon as they discover she can hardly spin at all, how everyone will laugh at her – she will be cast out of this Paradise! Then a strange, small, rumpled man appears. 'Tears trickle down your cheeks, child,' he says. 'Tell me your affliction.' So Rosanie does.

'Take hold of the end of my wand,' the man says at last. It is made of an unspecified wood and garnished with a changeable stone, the pinkish red of a carnelian. 'Touch this to hemp or flax,' he instructs. 'It will spin as much as you like, even the finest silk like Arachne! I will lend it to you for three months, but this is my condition – when I come back you must say: "Well, Ricdin-Ricdon, here is your wand." If you cannot remember my name, I will own you.' The name seems so easy to remember she accepts at once. Soon the queen is admiring some lovely textiles, and, of course, Prince Lovejoy and Rosanie fall in love.

But then this, perhaps, is where Télésille's story diverges from the version you know. She introduces the character of Bleakthought, who has some beauty and ambition and 'a black soul, in equal parts cunning and vindictive'. Spurned by the prince, Bleakthought visits a witch in order to reap a terrible vengeance. Soon, the prince is informed that a cruel tyrant called Hollowdream has taken over the neighbouring realm of Fiction and that he should marry the Princess of Fiction, for political reasons, but when – faithful to Rosanie – he rejects her advances, she is revealed as a demon-lover.

Bleakthought is furious her plan has failed, so next arranges to have Rosanie abducted. Fortunately, Rosanie is able to escape her kidnapper. Now nothing should be able to get in the way of these two young hearts becoming husband and wife, except. Except. Oh, what is that man's name?

Hopeful that writing might help her to recover the name that has so slipped from her mind, Rosanie scrawls down:

Racdon
Ricordon
Ringaudon
Raccledon
Rippleride
Rumpeldon
Ricci-ticci
Rattletattle
Rumpelskin

Luckily, the prince, out at night, passes a ruined old palace, all its windows broken, in which – by the glimmer of violet flames, as at a witches' sabbat – he sees a

strange, desiccated, cheerful little man making leaps and
bounds and singing:

> In the morning she is mine,
> What a shame, what a shame,
> Silly girl, self to blame,
> Beautiful but not that bright.
> Ricdin-Ricdon is my name.
> Can't remember? What a shame.

Anyway, it turns out that Rosanie is the true princess
of the realm of Fiction, who was said to be a stillbirth
(there is some business with pâté), then smuggled out in
a coffin to the rustic cottage, to protect her from the
tyrant. You can tell by a birthmark the perfect design of
a rose on her elbow.

On her wedding day, Ricdin-Ricdon appears, but
thanks to her husband's superior memory, Rosanie can
say, 'Well, Ricdin-Ricdon, here is your wand,' and the evil
spirit howls and is swallowed up by the earth. They all
live happily ever after.

Well, except for Bleakthought, who kills the witch,
then kills herself in a murder-suicide.

'Bravo!' Madame d'Aulnoy says, as it ends, clapping.
This time she must admit that Télésille has displayed
some real talent. Has she been judging her too harshly?
Surely one of Reynie's flies would not have introduced a
witch into their tale? Unless it is a double bluff, intended
to throw them off the scent. The rest of the audience
clap too, as Télésille curtseys and blushes.

'So original!' Charles says. 'And yet the ancient spirit

of the troubadours seemed to flow through you too, dear cousin, as you hoped – very well done. I can quite imagine Blondel singing of such things to Richard the Lionheart in the Third Crusade. You have earned your place on Mount Parnassus.'

'And the moral?' the Princesse de Conti slurs, remarkably still conscious, although she didn't really focus except for the bit with the penis-wand.

'The moral is, of course, not to lightly make dangerous engagements.'

'Oh yes? Yes, sensible. What a very very sensible romance you've written! That's all of us told.'

'Sorry?' Télésille asks, her face dropping; a baffled, devastated look coming over her face.

'But if Rosanie hadn't made the dangerous engagement, she would have been sent in failure back to the rude cottage,' Charlotte-Rose observes, from behind her carefully posed fan, for she is gaining a little more confidence now in the art of critique. 'There would have been no adventures. She would never have discovered she was a princess in the realm of Fiction.'

'Perhaps the moral should be: always remember the names of your enemies!' Charles suggests, with faux-casualness (how he would like, though, to know the names of his).

'I shall certainly remember the name Bleakthought now, there is a lady at court I shall inwardly apply it to,' Charlotte-Rose notes. 'I loved the bit with the witches' sabbat too. Utterly chilling.'

'Rici-Ricdoo was more of a goblin, I think,' Charles

blusters, keen to steer it away from witches. 'Sorry, Ricdee-Racdee, was it?' The salon laughs. This is distraction, he knows perfectly well.

'King Prudent and Queen Laborious,' the princess snorts. 'Ha! That really is true fantasy! Imagine a queen that works. That can clean her own teeth, even! Imagine my father acting with care for anything or anyone—'

Charles and Marie meet eyes then, at this explicit reference to the princess's parents. Marie looks as calm as ever but he can see the fear, somehow, all the same, pulsing in her brow. He swallows. 'Another tale, I think,' he suggests, brightly. 'So much to get through. Is it me next, Madame d'Aulnoy? I only have a little peasant tale this evening, a rustic mere squib, but I hope it will amuse . . .' She nods at him, eagerly.

It is the one with the three foolish wishes.

In it Jupiter, the god, unexpectedly gives a woodcutter three wishes. That night, celebrating over a glass of wine, he accidentally wishes for a black pudding, which crawls out of the chimney like an awful snake. When his wife screams at him for idiocy, he ends up losing his temper and wishing the black pudding was hanging from the end of her nose. His final wish has to be that her nose returns to its original condition.

It is not one of Charles's best. In fact, truth be known, he has barely changed a word of the story from the one his nurse told him, and the tale's chief merit is that it contains no kings, queens or witches whatsoever. Still it gets a few filthy laughs, especially from some marquis at the back – one who he does not remember seeing previously, except at the dressing ceremony of the king in Versailles, deepening Charles's unease. He only hopes he is providing a suitable diversion.

What would he wish now?

To be back at the heart of Versailles? Perhaps. No, not that.

For his wife to be alive again?

But he knows how such stories work: how her dead body would rise up, rotting, anguished, all her sweetness gone. How she would long to be dead again. Or no, he would not be able to believe it was her: she would seem some demon-lover come to trick him. It could never be the same. He would have to wish her back into the grave.

Charles wishes he could help Marie d'Aulnoy. Reach out to her, somehow, as a close friend. He would like to squeeze her hand, he thinks, suddenly, although only if she would find such a thing tolerable. He wishes . . . Does he wish to kiss her? The thought disturbs him. No, it seems too coarse, she would not want to. He won't admit that thought, he wants simply – doesn't he? – to connect with another human being. To see them and be seen by them. *I wish. I wish.*

And then Berthe appears at the door, and whispers something into Madame d'Aulnoy's ear, and she is shaking her head, and a little buzz of consternation travels through the crowd. Slowly, stooping slightly, Reynie walks in.

'Well well well,' he says. 'The famous salon of Madame d'Aulnoy.' He takes off his hat. 'You are the fays are you, ladies and gentlemen? The Modern Fairies. Les précieuses. What a precious little scene this is, isn't it?'

'Good evening, Reynie,' Charles says, instinctively taking charge, his sense being that Reynie responds better to men. 'What bad wind brings you here to disturb the evening of these people?'

'Oh, I am very sorry about that,' Reynie says, blinking his brown lids indolently. 'Yes, it's just I've been very busy with pickpockets and vagrants and brothels and so on. Paris never sleeps, Perrault, especially the lowlifes, and so I've only just found time to deliver this lettre de cachet, but I do like to deliver them all personally, coming, as they do, directly from His Royal Highness our king Louis XIV – I consider it a great honour. This one's for . . .' He squints at the letter and then reads the full name out, as if enjoying the taste of every syllable. 'Charlotte-Rose Caumont de La Force. If you could show yourself, I've been told to take you to the Benedictine abbey of Gercy-en-Brie.'

'I am she,' Charlotte-Rose says, in a clear, quavering voice, stepping forward.

'If you'll come with me, you can collect some of your things first, madame, although I believe you'll have no use for beauty patches and fans and other such female fripperies in a convent.'

'No!' Marie d'Aulnoy cries out. 'No! She's done nothing wrong. It was the boy's family. The marriage was signed off by the king.'

Angélique lays down her fan, and rushes to put her arm around Charlotte-Rose for support. Having thought the lettre de cachet was surely her own, she is shaky and slightly hysterical. 'Oh, darling girl, those awful men. We can't let them!' Charlotte-Rose herself seems to stand there very still, teetering, detached, as though she is watching herself act out a story. She can't quite believe this is happening to her: that she is going to be locked up far far away from male company amongst the celibate, as if caught in her own plot.

Reynie tuts. 'Calm down, ladies, please. It says here it's for more literary reasons – the king just doesn't like the word "poison", you see. He doesn't understand why a morally improving children's story – if indeed those are what you perform on these evenings, which stretches my credulity, I must say – needs to include nasty little words like "poison".'

'Who told you?' Marie asks, a phrase that comes out half-hiss.

'Just a little fly on the windowsill. You know –' He speaks to her more softly, privately now. 'A little word of advice, Marie-Catherine: I always say, now you're in Paris, it's easiest to just assume the king sees and knows everything. That way, you'll always be on your best behaviour, won't you? And you know that the king takes a particular interest in the company *you* keep, madame, don't you? A very particular interest.' She nods meekly. She had forgotten, just then, to conceal her feelings.

As Reynie walks Charlotte-Rose out into the hallway, Charles hurries after him, putting what he has heard between Reynie and Marie aside – unable to think through its ramifications just yet. 'Wait,' he says near the door. 'Stop for a moment, please. What is this, Reynie? You're truly arresting Charlotte-Rose for the word "poison"? Exiling a young woman, with her future ahead of her, as though that word is not on everyone's lips? As though it doesn't obsess you too? Who is the story meant to offend: Athénaïs, your enemy?'

'I said she was your enemy, Perrault, not mine. The king has asked for a freeze on all legal papers relevant to Athénaïs, and her name is to be excised from the court dossier, to avoid any further scandal. I have sentenced thirty-four people to death and La Voisin will burn, but the trial of Athénaïs will not happen now. No. Thanks to cowards like you, she still has some influence at court, and the enormity of her crimes has proven to be her safeguard. Those of you who attend this salon would do well to remember that before you mock her.'

'Just fairy tales, Reynie! You do this, then, to punish me?'

'Oh, you are not so important as that any more, Charles Perrault,' Reynie says, as he walks Charlotte-Rose out of the door.

For a few moments after they have left the building, there is an embarrassed, painful hush in Marie's fine coral room. A sniff. A click of tongue. Someone's stomach growls. 'I do not want to say I told you so,' the abbé squeaks at last, strangely, to the remaining salonnières, his eyes puffy with emotion, tugging at his waxen locks. 'But you cannot say I have not been pointing out, for many weeks, the wicked pagan undertones of these contes de fées, which were always likely to get women such as yourselves into trouble. Although your minds are an ornament of Paris, one does wonder if you should focus yourselves on occasional verse, Bible study and homemaking, rather than cross-dressing wolves and such-forth. I am not so naive as to be unaware that people in this city have mocked my cheerful little poems about lavender-coloured carriages and other light-hearted diversions! But at least they aren't ungodly, lewd or treasonous. Well, I've said my piece.'

The glass of wine in Marie's hand trembles for a moment, such is her urge to toss it in his face, but, instead, she opts to take pity on this man.

Perrault does not. Anger overtakes him, surging through his blood. What is this bilious soliloquy, if not the confession of their fly? Surely it proves it is he! 'What a nasty little speech, abbé,' he snaps bitterly. 'No, don't tell me, was it by the playwright Molière?'

20. The Tale of the Mirror

The problem with mirrors is ourselves.

Athénaïs stares at herself in the looking glass: her creamy face, with its fine cheekbones and dimples, has put on weight – she knows the court wit, Primi Visconti, last week dared to say that one of her legs was as thick as his own thigh – and her jowls are heavier somehow, despite her endless massages in the vanilla-steam of the baths.

Her ice-blue eyes, that once caused such damage to men's hearts, seem slightly buried and swollen, and have lost their shine, whilst her eyebrows have become scanty too – she should perhaps order a false set made of mouse-skin.

Athénaïs's own skin is blackening in spots on her cheek, which she covers up with thick white-lead powder, not realizing her solution is the cause, and also infecting her eyes. There is a new little wart on her chin, so she conceals that now with a gummed-on beauty patch shaped like a star.

Still, her thousand blonde ringlets still surround her face, don't they, in that style called the hurluberlu – meaning eccentric – held just so with a pomade of lard, that she has made famous. She wonders aloud: 'Am I the fairest in the land?'

No, my queen, the mirror responds.

Louis has had her name removed from the trial papers, but she can see that he is angry with her, for damaging his carefully wrought image; tarnishing his golden sun. Does she have, any more, the allure to win him back on to her side? She feels exhausted; dreary. And after all these years, does she even have the will – for who is he, really, that she loves him so much? Short, pockmarked, always some problem with his arsehole; the food bubbling out of his mouth into his nose, that grim spring, as he ravages some greasy little carcass; his little dick florid with some new sexually transmitted infection; pockets full of dog biscuits. Oh God, and his ludicrous high-heeled shoes wind her up so much. How she has had to hold her sharp tongue, from mocking him! The king, such a pathetic little horn-dog he even fucked her maid whilst she was in the bath. He is ageing now too: the gout; sciatica; the constant bleedings and enemas. They say that the Spanish king can only digest human milk.

Does she love Louis or hate him? Did she ever love him? Or was it only his power; his crown; his throne; the parties; the sparkle; how her reflection looked when they fucked in the Hall of Mirrors, and she was on top?

Madame de Maintenon has his ear now. Maintenon! They are calling her his new official mistress. That governess, who *she herself* set up in the Rue de Vaugirard in Paris with a large income and staff, so Maintenon could bring up their illegitimate children – hers and Louis's – discreetly. And now that holier-than-thou schoolmarm is turning his head with talk about Christ and redemption

197

and banning opera during Lent. In the corridors of Versailles they are punning on her name, calling her Madame Now!

And as for his libido, well. There is another little girl, for she saw him at the last ball, drooling. The girl reminded her of someone, like a tiny ghost. But does Athénaïs have the appetite, really? There is no La Voisin to help her now; her inheritance powders are all used up. What would it win her, to end that girl's life? A few more months, plus maybe a charitable fuck or two for old times' sake, before she's pushed into some convent to repent her ways, as Louis's women always are, in the end, with one more sin to atone for. Oh God, was she always just another of his women?

. . . Louise, Bonne, Diane, Thérèse, Catherine, Julie, Anne-Madeleine, Gabrielle, Marie, Isabelle, Lydie, Olympia . . .

The story is meant to end when the king falls in love with you; why has it never ended, why has she had to win him again and again and again? Why don't they tell you it is the beautiful princess who becomes the evil queen; that they are just the same person at different points in their story?

Athénaïs drags rouge powder across her cheeks with a wad of wool; daubs on a lipstick made of animal fat and beetroot. *There. That's better. Come on, you can do this.*

'I am the fairest of them all,' she affirms into the mirror.

Not you, my queen, the mirror replies. *Not any more.*

The problem with mirrors is ourselves.

21. The Tale of the Ballgown

Judith d'Aulnoy has chosen a blue-green dress, the colour of celadon porcelain, that looks very striking against her auburn hair. Françoise d'Aulnoy, who has opted for lavender, has just been discovered to have nits, and so her nurse, Mimi, is picking them out as best she can with a fine comb whilst Françoise stands there with a dreamy grin on her face.

'What are you thinking of, my hen?' Mimi asks.

'I'm just imagining everyone in the whole room falls in love with me. It's pretty awkward.'

'Number thirty!' Mimi says, holding one up. 'Is that a record?'

'I had fifty-two once,' Françoise says. 'Belle-Belle actually picked one out of my hair and ate it! No really, she actually did!' The monkey, Belle-Belle, is eating a bruised red-and-green apple now, on the sideboard, her little side-burned cheeks chomping furiously.

Thérèse, the middle daughter, appears suddenly in red. It suits her very much, her new breasts apparent; her thin dark hair is pinned back, so you can see her oval face; her small round mouth. 'Girls, are you ready?' Marie is saying. 'The coachman is outside – oh! Oh, Thérèse.'

Another daughter is almost a young woman. 'Will you not come too, Maman?'

'I think it is not wise. My reputation has been higher. Oh, Thérèse, you look – just. So.' A vertiginous feeling comes over her, as though she might drop over the edge of the world.

rose   red   snow   white   rose   red   snow   white
rose   red   snow   white   rose   red   snow   white

'Maman?'

'I have a migraine,' Marie manages, which is a sort of truth. 'I'm so sorry, girls. Please, enjoy your evening. Be courteous, be careful, don't stay out too late, look after each other.' She wishes that she was a mother who kissed her children as a habit, so that she could kiss them farewell now, as if it might be a kind of protective magic.

In the meantime, elsewhere in the city, Angélique Tiquet is also preparing for the ball with more care than usual. It doesn't begin until 11 p.m. and is expected to go on until morning, so it always pays to dine beforehand, and Angélique is therefore enduring a rather strained dinner with her husband, Claude, each of them at separate ends of a long table. Recently they have mainly kept to their own wings of the house, but she has given him a great deal of money this week in order to placate him. There are all the usual courses of soup, eggs, fish and meat served up on gold and silver plate in the dim, flickering light.

Claude does not wear his wig at home and has a wholly bald head, although hair covers his body, making dark wings of fuzz on his back. He is a strong, stolid type, though his eyes have always seemed a little too large for their sockets. Angélique has asked Moura to put the poison she has obtained into the mutton with gravy and garlic, as that is a dish Claude loves that she herself always avoids, it sitting too heavily in her stomach. In fact, all the meat is a bit much, to be honest, every day: she'd live on dessert if she could.

It is such a beautiful room that she has made, she thinks: the bas-reliefs; floral silk summer curtains; the marble console table; the Gobelins tapestry of the Rape of Europa; the vases of lilies. She loves beauty. Why should this man think he can marry her and then take all her beautiful things?

The trouble is, she is not confident there is quite enough arsenic, or that Claude will eat quite enough – he's barely had a forkful. The plan is for her to go to the ball – so she won't be there when her husband dies, and can feign surprise – but the valet, Moura, is on orders to keep an eye on Claude, and if it seems he's only half-dead or stumbles for help or some such thing, she has given him a gun to finish Claude off. They will say it was a robbery: there are so many robberies now, since the bad harvest.

'More wine?' Moura asks, very formally, holding the jug – painted with dancing bacchantes – a little towel over his arm.

'Please, please,' Angélique says in her most charming voice, smiling up at him. 'Oh, Claude, you must want some more too, such an excellent Beaujolais grape, I imagine it really goes well with the mutton, what a shame I can't try that combination.'

Claude hates her voice – how grossly apparent it is when she's trying to please a man – but mistakes himself for the man she wants to please. When she gave him the money that he asked for, he took it as a sign that she is willing to make further concessions. Now it seems that she really imagines he might find her desirable again, pouting with that grey, stinking mouth. 'Fine, yes, top me up, Moura.'

Moura, we might notice, is quite handsome for an eighteen-year-old valet, in a kind of unfinished, elongated way – long skinny body, long face – that makes his friends at the inn call him 'the Baguette'. There is a line of thought that his nickname has a further source as well, as Angélique discovered last week, when, as a little thank you for his recent help, she tried to fit his penis in her mouth and ended up making really unpleasant gagging noises that startled Madame Miaou (who stood rigid, with her tail up stiff and growled at him). Thoughtfully, Moura rectified the situation by pulling her up on to the side of the bed instead. He got on his knees then and pushed deep, deep inside of her – young hungry thrusts – until she saw the ceiling spin.

'I didn't pull out in time, madame,' he mumbled afterwards, getting dressed. Slightly nervous, almost as though he wanted to do a little dance. Hormonal spots still blotching the corner of his handsome mouth. 'I'm sorry if I was meant to. I'm sorry if I was too quick for you – I was just—'

'No, no,' she smiled, 'don't worry, I can sort that out,

Moura. We're helping each other out, aren't we? Two friends.'

There is a mewl under the table, so Claude moves to pick up a scrap of mutton. 'Here, Madame Miaou, here!'

Angélique yelps. The cat scurries to her lap. 'Fish for you today,' she says, palpitating, trying to peel the bone off the sole. 'Better for your tum. My, it's warm this evening, isn't it? Well. I suppose that I had better get ready for that ball. Are you sure you won't come, Claude?'

'No,' he says. 'All those preening women, it sets my teeth on edge. I feel out of sorts anyway.'

So she gets dressed, Angélique, in a brocaded taffeta puff-sleeved dress with a bright blue sash, pearls at the neck and white lace gloves. She climbs into the horse-drawn carriage, a footman stood on the little step at the back. Moura nods calmly to her from the window as she leaves, filling her with reassurance and a sense of great euphoria – she feels positively young again.

Oh, she is off to a grand ball at Versailles, what a lark!

And you may go to the ball too, reader. We are here, on this late-summer evening, and isn't it a wonderful thing to witness? There is a wild, carnival atmosphere. Please make a short and witty remark as you are introduced to the Dauphin and Dauphine. Everywhere there are oranges hanging from the trees, those plump suns, and so many flowers – jasmine's constellations blooming beneath the starry sky, perfuming the night air; a carpet of jonquils. Sweets, wines and liqueurs laid out for guests to help themselves.

Everyone is air-kissing. Men bow and laugh. The women in their dresses are like flowers too, are they not, in every colour – dipping and twirling, flirting and fanning in their endless dance, in and out of rooms, the grottos and canopies. So many wigs, made out of the finest Norman country-women's hair, powdered with flour, scented with bergamot. Wigs poufed up over iron frames, padded out with horsehair; so tall that their owners have to bend to go through doorways. One seems to be decorated with fruit; another appears to have a rat peeking out of it.

And here is the new Salle de Bal, with its semicircular cascading fountain; its gilded torch lamps – the perfect backdrop for a summer's dance party. The court orchestra have struck up, the greatest composer of the age Jean-Baptiste Lully amongst them. There are some faces here you might recognize: there is Angélique, dancing with a middle-aged man, a Baron something, in a way that speaks of a previous intimacy, her smile glitching with distraction. And Judith dances with a boy her own age, who makes excruciating small talk about the moon. The Princesse de Conti leans against a pedestal as her husband tries to recall the lines for that theatre-piece they occasionally perform, in which they are married. Little Françoise's fancy new shoes don't quite fit – she is more used to being barefoot, truth be told – and one has flayed a tiny patch of skin off her heel, which the blood blots through. She is standing at the side of the dance floor inspecting it, when she looks up and her mouth falls open.

Oh: many people, in fact, seem to be staring at a couple on the floor now. There, even, is Athénaïs with her hangers-on: her face frozen and cracked, like its own reflection in a broken mirror.

The king, you see – Louis XIV, the Sun King himself – is dancing a gavotte with a mysterious young woman dressed in scarlet. The young woman has skin as white as snow, hair black as ebony, and lips like blood.

The bell tolls for midnight.

22. The Tale of Puss-in-Boots

The scandalous story that follows has been told many times.

The poison didn't work, or only enough to give Claude a measure of diarrhoea and terrible abdominal pain that he found very suspicious, so he decided to go out to see his friend for a second opinion – a doctor who lived on the next street – but was shot three times in the back. As he crawled along the filthy gutter, he glimpsed a tall, slim and ultimately familiar silhouette in the shadows. Unfortunately or fortunately, depending on your perspective, and certainly slightly embarrassingly, this shooting was also botched. Though one pellet was later found near his heart, Claude survived. It is well known that when passers-by found him, he moaned the words: 'Do not take me back to my own house, for I have no enemy but my own wife.'

Angélique was immediately the main suspect, then. A witness was also said to have overheard her telling a friend: 'It is impossible for me to have any enjoyment of myself whilst my husband lives. His health is too good for me to look for a quick revolution of fortune.'

Angélique Tiquet was never likely to endure the water-torture. It was the custom, in those days, to stretch the suspect out on a rack and force eight pots of water down their gullet, and Angélique always did have a strong gag-reflex. She only endured one pot before, having calculated her inability to withstand the procedure, she confessed practically everything, giving up her accomplice Moura as well.

Marie d'Aulnoy looks a mess when she is granted permission to visit Angélique in the Bastille; hollowed out by sleeplessness. Firstly, the girls came home at six in the morning from the ball, all talking at once: Françoise pretending to have lost a slipper, for some attention; Judith reeling off the names of boys. And Thérèse, most disturbingly, stood there with that radiant and terrible clarity in her red dress, as Iphigenia must have stood before the crowd at Aulis.

Then, after dawn the next day, Marie heard the terrible news of Angélique's arrest and so many memories came flooding back. This time she could not stop the deluge; it knocked her over. Oh, those two men who her mother persuaded to accuse the baron of tax evasion! Charles Bonenfant and Jacques de Crux. Bonenfant, most of all. How did she allow him, moved by pity for her situation, to get caught up, somehow, in her mother's elaborate ruse to change their fortunes – that awful game of spillikins? They hadn't even slept together when it began, but he had wanted to save her; his head turned by such romantic notions. How bitterly Marie regrets that night she cried and he kissed the wet lids of her eyes, oh God, sweet stupid man! She so longed to be saved, she let him think that he might save her! But he was not saving her, she was dooming him, with her dewy lashes, her soft shivers, her vulnerability.

After the baron was imprisoned, she and Bonenfant had played, tentatively, privately, at being a family. Simple dinners. At first, trauma made her rigid to touch, but he was patient and gentle, and at last they made love; woke up together, naked in crumpled bedding. He would massage her back when she was pregnant. How much care he lavished on their newborn, little Judith, singing the babe to sleep! But Marie knew somehow that it was all makeshift; cursed. And then the baron had his sentence overturned, and when she heard the news she vomited.

And now Angélique is locked up in the Bastille, the place from Marie's nightmares – how often she dreams of the baron in there, goading her, his long yellow teeth protruding from the grey-streaked beard, licking his lips like a wolf, writing filthy letters about what he will do to her when he gets out. And then it is not him, he has changed into Bonenfant, her good young man who has barely lived and wants to live so much: who is pleading with his captor for just one more dreg of life.

How can she forgive herself for escaping punishment, when Bonenfant was killed for the same crime? How can she forgive herself for clambering down the rope of tied-together bedclothes from that turret, her mother waiting impatiently at the bottom, as if she scarcely believed what her own maternal conscience was making her do. Baby Judith was bound too tightly to Marie's chest, so she kept worrying she was crushing her; milk leaking like hot shame through the fabric. And then her lover was executed whilst she was on that midnight flight on a lurching, flea-ridden boat to England. To Saint-Évremond, shelter and gin.

The year after that, she fled to Germany, when she thought Louis's men were on to her. Later, onwards to Spain. A decade sliding through her fingers. Strange cooking oils upsetting their stomachs; long, feverish journeys; a flash flood; the years a fever-dream. Her baby girl going limp in that Madrid hotel room. And Marie always on watch, fully alert; signing false names; incognito; shuddering when a hand touched her shoulder. Afraid of drinking water. Afraid of smallpox. Afraid of the king or the baron or any man, in truth, with an opinion about wives. Never able to rest until that letter from Saint-Évremond found her, with an offer he had brokered from Versailles – a deal that included forgiveness, a fine house in Paris (how she longed for Paris!) and a pension, in exchange for her provision of a service.

'Am I selling my soul?' she had asked her friend in reply. Saint-Évremond had written that it was possible, but all things considered, also probably the best price she'd get for it in this life.

For two nights now she has not slept, but lain clawing at her skull: Françoise's head lice perhaps, hopping in her hair like bad thoughts. She should let Mimi groom her with the fine-tooth comb, but she shirks from it: from sitting, as a girl, between Mimi's legs, gripped by Mimi's warm body, which she suckled from. Too many memories forced down her gullet, she cannot bear them.

The Bastille is the embodiment of royal power: brutal

and heedless. A vast medieval fortress with eight towers, its ditches fed by the Seine. Guards watch Marie d'Aulnoy approach from the crenellated walkway. Detention here is by direct order from the king, and so indefinite and shrouded in secrecy – there is rumour that a man in an iron mask has been held here for decades in a cell with multiple doors, one closing upon another, though no one knows why (some whisper that it is Louis XIV's older, illegitimate brother, or his secret biological father). Most here are nobles; many are imprisoned simply for being troublesome, or as a favour to Louis's friends. Marie finds herself shaking with nerves as she passes over the drawbridge and beneath the jaws of the portcullis: it is like entering a huge storm-cloud, a mass of suppressed dark energy that will one day burst and sweep away all of Paris. She is led down grey corridors. The richest prisoners have manservants, who are imprisoned with their masters, slumped over their lightless tasks. Someone screams; someone waves their penis; someone is being stuffed into a straitjacket.

Up the stone staircase, in her cell, Angélique looks strange without her make-up. Almost unrecognizable, although still you can see the beauty in a ruined masterpiece. 'I'm so glad they let you come for one last visit! You were right, Marie,' she says, in a soft hoarse drawl. 'You really were. I just wanted to say that. You know what, though? I'm glad they're going to kill me, no really, I am. I just don't think this is the kind of place I'd like to live in for very long, it isn't me – it's so mouldy, and there's no sherbets or champagne, no sparkle at all.

There's no – no beauty! And that's what I've lived for, Marie. Passion and beauty. Tell them that, won't you, at the salon, Marie – our friends? Tell them I always did live for passion and beauty.'

'Of course,' Marie says, thinking that there can be no harm, now, at this late stage, in allowing Angélique to edit the story of her life. 'You did.'

'Will you look after Madame Miaou, please, she's going' – Angélique sobs then, the thought ripping off the mask of her brave face – 'she's going to miss me so much, my darling puss. She needs so much fuss, you see, so many cuddles, and she'll think I don't love her! She'll think I've deserted her, but I never would, I never would—'

'I know,' Marie says, as the tears rain down. 'I promise. She'll be safe with me forever.'

When Marie returns to the house with Madame Miaou, whom she has picked up from Angélique's neighbour in the carriage, she releases the cat on to the floor and it scampers straight towards the fire and Mimi's lap.

Why do the words of the witness who condemned Angélique come back into Marie's mind now? *It is impossible for me to have any enjoyment of myself whilst my husband lives.* Something about a revolution of fortune. And these words, why do they possess, suddenly, such an unpleasant tang of familiarity? A thought flushes through her; a horrible hot sensation.

Instead of waiting for Berthe, Marie hurries to take off her own coat and hang it in the cloakroom, checking, as she does so, the peg beside it where her loup usually hangs. On seeing her black velvet mask is missing, Marie pauses for a moment, letting the knowledge settle, before she gives a little nod; gulps some disappointment down.

'Hello, little kitty,' Mimi is saying in the front room, holding out her knuckle to Madame Miaou, who sniffs it and then gently gnaws it. 'Oh, a little cat kiss for me, is it?' Mimi tickles her white belly. 'They don't care about us really, you know. They like anyone who feeds them.'

'Well, she likes you.'

'The children have just gone to bed,' Mimi tells Marie. 'Although I don't think they're sleeping, to be honest. When I left them Thérèse and Françoise were playing at being moles under the blankets.'

'Did you tell them one of your stories, Mimi?'

'Yes, they asked for "Puss-in-Boots" tonight. I think your friend Charles has a new version, but we like it the old way, like in the book by that Italian fellow Basile you used to have as a little one, where the cat is a girl-cat – they call her Your Pussyship, I like that! They couldn't ask for a better cat, could they? The way she uses her guile to get her humans good clothes and food. But then after all that work, when they think her dead they only say: "Take her by the leg and fling her out of the window."'

'You always told that version so well,' Marie says, sitting down beside her.

'Why, thanks, ma petite crotte. And the cat, who turns out not to be dead after all, says: "Such is the fate of one who washes an ass's head! You are not worth spitting in the face!" And she throws her cloak around her and goes her way.'

'I think you're calling me an ass,' Marie says softly, looking into the flames, though they make her eyes smart. 'But that's all right, really, Mimi, I think perhaps I am. You are Reynie's fly, I realize that now.'

'Oh, nonsense,' Mimi says, with a strained chuckle and so little conviction that Marie continues as if she has just confessed.

'Only you could have heard Angélique's words to me after the salon! *His health is too good for me to look for a quick revolution of fortune.* She said that to me because she thought she was safe here. But you were sat by the fire, listening in. You borrowed my mask, I suppose, for your assignations.'

'When you're a nurse, you see,' Mimi explains, slowly, pinkening, a tremor in her voice – almost as much to herself as to Marie, the speech clearly pre-rehearsed in her mind – 'you're one of the family, but you're really not. It's just a job, for money. And they can fire you, just like that – like your father did to me – and no one even says goodbye. You were my little heart, and you never even said goodbye.'

'I—' Marie begins. Can it be that she remembers it wrongly? Was she the one with more power in that relationship, after all? How horrifying, this second truth.

'Your father was such an awful prick!' Mimi cries out, her wrinkled eyes suddenly bright and dancing.

'Yes, he was,' Marie agrees, and the women smile, timidly, hopefully, at each other.

213

'I wouldn't harm you, you know, Marie,' Mimi adds, poking the fire as she settles into her performance. Tiny sparkles shoot from the log. 'I know you do your best with the cards you've been dealt. You've an interesting mind, I've always thought so. I was so glad when you invited me here, that you remembered me fondly after all those years! And the children – my girls! I do love children. But the women at your salon – I'm sorry, but I don't feel for them, I don't. Just – just stealing tales off working women like me and my mum and my gran, generations of women, all those Mother Geese loving and caring and warning each other. And they just fancy it up with hundreds of diamonds and some posh classical-sounding names and make out like they're saving modern literature! They think they're better than us, but that letter from the princess to Henriette de Murat was complete filth – I got Belle-Belle to steal that for me, she's a handy little monkey, she is, naturally stealthy. And that Charlotte-Rose, she can't even pass a puddle without admiring herself. Télésille too! She's who I'd got in my mind to give to Reynie next. What did she say? Stories fill with impurities as they pass through common people, like water through a dirty culvert! Pardon my French, but what a fucking bitch.'

'She shouldn't have said that,' Marie admits, glad that Mimi has so many excuses, for she does not want to stop loving her.

'I tried not to mention Charles Perrault much, because you like him.'

'Do I?'

'Yes, Marie.' For a moment, Marie sits with this new fact about herself. But then she feels the anger rising in her chest – how can Mimi be so self-righteous after what she has done; so lacking in empathy for their friends? She hasn't even offered a word of apology!

'I visited Angélique today,' Marie tells her, more sharply, trying to prompt a flash of guilt.

'Who is a *murderer*! Oh, come on. She can't even tell stories, that one. Tell me why I shouldn't be glad to go and watch her head chopped off?' There is a long moment of silence. Mimi knows she's gone too far again, although she's too bursting with all the pent-up years, now, to say sorry.

'But spying on me, Mimi!' Marie yelps, indignantly. 'Really? For that – that *man*! If you needed money, you could have come to me.'

'Don't give me one of those foolish morals.'

'It's not foolish to try and be moral! I mean, I know we get it wrong sometimes, but. "No man is clever enough to know all the evil he does." That's Rochefoucauld. I often think of it.'

'Oh, that is a very good one, to be fair. What do you mean by it, though, is that me or you?'

'All of us!' Marie tells her, for Mimi really is unbelievable.

'I know you look after me all right, Marie, but I have family – brothers, sisters, nieces, a stepdaughter. I even had a husband for a time, though I mislaid him. Not that you lot ever ask me about them and how they are. It's been a hard winter, hasn't it, for working folk? Why shouldn't I use my brains and tongue to profit, like you do, eh? There's babies froze to death out there. My stepdaughter has this lovely little baby, just – the smell of the top of her head, why shouldn't she have a warm shawl just because she wasn't born to a dame? I love babies.'

'I know. They frighten me.'

'Two, was it, you lost? I lost three. All three.'

'I'm sorry,' Marie says, because she knew that, yet she's never allowed herself to think of it – for it is difficult, when you refuse to pity yourself, not to end up pitiless towards others too. 'I'm sorry that I never spoke of it with you.'

Mimi nods the tears back into her eyes, and tickles the cat under its throat, so it purrs with pleasure. 'Well, I'm sorry too, then,' she sniffs. 'You're right, he's not a nice man, that Reynie, something sinister about him, how he's always washing his hands. How he says "bzzzzzt bzzzt".'

'It's not fair, though, you're right. None of it's fair.'

'There'll be a revolution one of these days, mark my words. People have had enough, and all your fancy friends will be on the wrong side, you know. Camels and needles and all that.'

'It's true. That's true. Mimi?'

'Yes?'

'Please don't throw your cloak around you and leave. I don't want to lose you again.'

'Not if you don't want me to, ma puce. Hey Marie' – Mimi puts Madame Miaou aside and pats the sofa between her legs – 'you've got lice, haven't you? I saw you scratching just then. Come here.'

216

'Oh, I'm fine,' Marie says, as is her habit.

'No, really though, you're not. Come here, my girl.'

And Marie comes and sits down between Mimi's thighs, to feel her old nurse pick up the comb and begin to tenderly rake her hair, lock by lock, pulling out each tiny, draining louse and squishing it between finger and thumb, and for the first time in such a long long time she weeps and weeps, as Mimi murmurs: 'Hush now, my little egg, there there.'

23. The Tale of the White Cat

Thousands crowd the streets at the Place de Grève.

A murmur travels through the crowd when they see Madame Angélique Tiquet and her valet appear. Moura looks like a broken man, limping and sobbing, whilst Angélique is elegant and sombre in black, her head held high. According to their social positions, the valet will hang first, before the main event in which the heiress has her head chopped off.

The dark grey clouds emit a grumble, as if some giant up there has a hungry stomach. A stalk of lightning. 'Proceedings delayed!' some jobsworth starts shouting over the wind. 'Proceedings delayed by a thunderstorm. REPEAT. PROCEEDINGS DELAYED BY A THUNDERSTORM!'

Grumble, CRACK!

Still, Angélique waits, the crowd must admit, with equanimity at the bottom of the scaffold until the storm passes, her cloak soaking through in the deluge, whilst Moura crouches and rubs his snot on the backs of his hands like an injured whelp. Thousands of Parisians, rich and poor, surge and boo beneath the whipping wetness; vendors try to sell their dilute beer and soggy souvenir biscuits; rushing waters rinse the streets. Some, who have climbed the famous lamp posts for a better view, now seem terribly exposed. Angélique's face is lit by the occasional flash: that sumptuous mouth – with a gap at the front now, the tooth finally gone – giving a faraway smile.

At last, when the storm eases to a drizzle, they hang Moura, who still appears to beg and snivel to his last breath. When the rope drops, his body jerks; the long face purples. The pressure on the cerebellum created by the noose also creates the condition of priapism, a phenomenon also known as a 'death erection' or 'angel lust', thus revealing to the crowd the 'Baguette' of legend. Many women, not to mention some men, who are stood there that day agree his death to be a pity.

At last, Angélique mounts the beams with poise and stagecraft, holding out her hand to the executioner for help to ascend the steps, then kneeling and seeming to say a silent prayer. After arranging her headdress, long hair and cleavage, she kisses the block.

'Sir,' she says to Longval, the executioner, 'might you be good enough to tell me the position I should take?'

'You have only to put your head on the block,' he replies. And Angélique obeys, as is her instinct.

'Is this all right, then?'

'Yes, that's good, madame.'

Her husband Claude watches from the front, with solemn satisfaction, stood next to Reynie, the chief of police. Abbé Cotin watches too, further back in the crowd, his cloak drawn over his nose. The others from the salon – what is left of them – do not want to watch, so are not amongst the teeming mob. Instead they are having a salon, of sorts, although it feels more like a funeral wake, at

Madame d'Aulnoy's house on the Rue Saint-Benoît. There is lots of champagne and lots of cake.

Briou has turned up, unexpectedly, looking sheepish, his head ducked a little as for a blow. Last night he had a wet dream about Angélique – in which he took her from behind as she bent over the executioner's block – that has made him feel obscurely sorry. All his hunting pals have gone to watch the big event, not knowing of his involvement with the accused, and when his invite from Marie arrived it seemed both a convenient excuse and the offer of atonement. The Princesse de Conti, who has been up all night gambling, pushes past him roughly as though on purpose on the way to her chair: 'Well, well, look who it is.'

'Good afternoon, Your Highness,' he replies, swallowing what he hopes is his medicine.

It may be the last salon for some time, Marie has warned them, now that Reynie is intensifying his crackdown on literary circles, and even private gatherings are no longer sacrosanct – royal licences for publishers, it's rumoured, have also dried up almost entirely. But she has a new fairy tale that she wants to share before it's over. It is called 'The White Cat'. You may know it.

The rain is lashing the windows. 'Once upon a time,' Madame d'Aulnoy begins – pausing a moment, for the grumble, CRACK of the storm to subside – 'a king, fearing that he would lose his throne to one of his three sons, set them an impossible task to distract them. He declared that whoever could obtain the smallest and most beautiful dog would be the next king, and gave them a year to obtain it.

'The youngest son travelled for some time, seeking small dogs, until one day he stumbled upon a fantastic castle hidden in the darkest part of the woods. Its walls, that seemed to be made of transparent porcelain, were painted with all the histories of the fairies from the beginning of time: Donkey-Skin was there, Cinderella, the Blue Bird, Persinette, the Subtle Princess, Ricdin-Ricdon, Anguillette and a hundred others. He tiptoed inside, and found a beautiful salon within, made of mother-of-pearl, lit by chandeliers and wax candles. Suddenly, bodiless hands appeared, that – noticing he'd got rather dirty on his travels – began to dress, powder and perfume him. In this salon, he perceived there were only pictures of famous cats – including Puss-in-Boots – and then several small cats appeared too, in an orchestra, and began to play miniature guitars. Was this a palace of cats?

'He observed a dinner table set with two places, and the bodiless hands pulled out a chair for him to sit down, before a beautiful white cat sat down opposite him. "How delightful to have company," she said. Their dinner was pigeon soup and baked mice, before he was shown to an apartment decorated by the feathers of rare birds. In the morning, when he looked out of the window, he saw the cats go off to hunt, chasing rabbits and birds whilst riding on the backs of monkeys.

'The youngest prince remained in the white cat's castle happily for nearly a year, enjoying her companionship, until the white cat reminded him of his mission and bestowed upon him an acorn. When he returned home and broke open the acorn, inside was an impossibly tiny dog, which danced a saraband with castanets.'

The salon laughs at that, though it is a strained laugh. A funereal laugh. Charles, who is holding Madame Miaou, gives Marie a little nod, as if to say: go on, you can do this. The rain is slowing to a speckle outside: a falling hush.

'Although the youngest prince was clearly the winner,' she continues, 'it was not a fair game. The king sent the princes out again, this time in search of muslin fine enough to be drawn through the eye of a needle. The youngest prince returned to the white cat's castle to spend another year there. At the end, she sent him home with a walnut, which contained magnificently embroidered muslin that fitted through the eye of any needle.

'Still, the king set a third task, telling them this time that whoever could find the most beautiful princess would be king. The youngest prince returned once more to the castle – unable to keep away from his beloved cat – and she promised to help him win the contest if he stayed.

'At the end of the year, the white cat told him that in order to find a beautiful princess, he needed to cut off her head.'

Marie takes a breath now. Perhaps she should imagine the room naked; count down from ten. The thing is not to think about the words too much, but just let them trot off your tongue.

'Her mother was a queen, you see,' she carries on. 'One of those queens who desperately crave a taste of that most delicate, delicious golden fruit that hangs in fairy gardens. In exchange, she promised her child away, as so many do. And the fairy cursed her, that child, to live as a white cat until someone was brave enough to free her.

'The prince at first refused to cut off his beloved cat's head, but she begged him to. She begged him and begged him. She wanted to be free. His sword trembled as he held it above her head . . .'

(No living person can, of course, be in all places at once, but I must interrupt Marie d'Aulnoy's tale to say that, legend has it, she read this bit out at the exact same moment that, in the Place de Grève, a heavy two-edged sword fell with its full weight on the neck of Angélique Tiquet. And there was a cry of horror then because blood spurted out – jets of it – but the head did not fall off. And the poor executioner, Longval, had to strike again but it was still not severed, so the cries of the crowd became threatening, until – blinded by blood that spurted at every stroke – he chopped down a third time in a kind of frenzy, and the head at last rolled off. Even after that, though, there were those who felt that the head of Madame Tiquet retained a kind of beauty. One spectator on the front row noted that: 'Nothing was more beautiful than her severed head.')

Marie's voice trembles as she ends her tale, all nerves, her smile fluttering with grief:

'So, the prince cut off his white cat's head, although he could hardly endure it. But he knew he had to do it to set her free; to allow her to become the ravishing queen she was always meant to be.'

24. The Tale of the Daughters

The salon over, Charles Perrault has stayed to help clear it away, gathering up his sad harvest of empty plates. 'Tell him it's all right, madame – you don't need to, honestly, sire, you don't,' Berthe says, making stop-him eyes at Marie, awkward with the male interference.

'It's no problem at all,' he says. 'Oh, the cake, Anne! That cake! Perhaps your most sublime yet. No, let me.' The girls share the leavings between them, as usual. Marie lets Charles stay. She will miss him, she realizes: his deep knowledge, his conversation, his little kindnesses. His lovely storyteller's voice.

There is a knock at the door, so she goes down to see. Belle-Belle has got hold of a sneaky glass of champagne; Françoise has a hula hoop. 'Not inside,' Mimi is saying.

When Marie comes back up the stairs, though, every muscle in her body is tense; part of her mind has flown to some dark elsewhere. Charles cannot help glancing through the window, where he sees a carriage outside – what looks like a royal carriage, with its distinct livery – and she is carrying a letter, he notices, with the king's fleur-de-lis. The veins on her neck are visible. 'Upstairs, girls,' she snaps. 'Out of my way, please, it's been a long afternoon, I want to speak to Monsieur Perrault privately.' Her daughters, tensing too, scatter.

Berthe, Anne, Mimi. All the women of the house except Marie, who presses the heavy door quietly shut and then looks at him.

The coral room is silent but for the creak of logs on the fire. Charles cannot think what it all means, except perhaps Marie is angry with him, which he finds he cannot bear – especially now, today, because he does not even know when he will see her again. He has stayed in the hope of spinning out a few more moments in her company, but she is livid, anyway, like one of the Erinyes.

'I want to apologize, madame – Marie, I mean,' he says, bumbling. I am, he thinks, truly a rambling old fool. 'I must confess that I was aware that Reynie had ill intentions directed at your salon. He came to me and asked for some assistance in a matter – a matter at Versailles – and I was cowardly. I have no taste, any more, to challenge the powerful – I am too afraid for myself, but my sons too, that is my excuse. I love them. And so it is safest to do nothing. And anyway, Marie, the truth is this: that when I refused him he – obscurely but I think distinctly – threatened this salon and all those who follow this fashion for contes de fées, as you yourself have, so brilliantly, christened them. He gave me the impression there was a spy in our midst, and—'

She says nothing. What is she thinking?

'And I should have confided in you,' he finishes. 'I wish that I had.'

'It is all right, Charles,' she says, after a pause, jerking her shoulders slightly, as if to shake something off. 'I know the identity of Reynie's spy, it is – was – one of my own household, I'm sorry to say, and I have dealt with them accordingly. It was really my responsibility.'

'Not the abbé? I thought that—'

'No, not him.'

'Ah. Perhaps I spoke rather harshly to him, then. Do you think I owe the fellow an apology? He has been rather maligned in polite society of late.'

'I shouldn't bother. You have nothing to apologize for, Charles, to him or to me, he quite deserved it. And I recognize what you say: I too have been afraid of the powerful – for myself and for my daughters. I still am, I think. I'm still too much that good girl who obeys. Who tells herself that those in charge must mean well.'

'Is it true, then?' he asks, something clarifying in his mind. 'I heard that – at the summer ball – the king danced with your daughter Thérèse.'

'It is his carriage waiting outside for her,' Marie replies, picking up someone else's half-drunk glass of champagne – perhaps the monkey's – and finishing it in a single gulp. 'There is a message. The king found her enchanting. He wants to see her again, for a private meeting in his rooms. The carriage will wait as long as it takes. That fucking piece of *shit.*' Her lip is curled up in a snarl, like some creature hurt too many times to pet. In a second, she throws the glass against the wall, trembling. 'THAT FUCKING PIECE OF SHIT!'

'What did he do to you?' Charles asks, urgently. She shakes her head, breathing hard.

'No, not me, not me, not me.'

'Who, then?' he asks.

'Do you remember another girl at Versailles called Thérèse?' Marie asks back.

And he does remember her, from soon after he arrived at the court: a doll-sized girl with white skin, red lips, black hair. Some little relative the king took a liking to, who he would let climb on his lap like a puppy. Louis indulged her with a little puppet theatre; let her sledge along the marble corridors of Versailles on trays. She had played at his feet. And then her tummy was swollen beneath her dress, which was very awkward, Colbert had told him, for everyone concerned. It hadn't even been known that she had commenced her monthly bleeding.

Perrault believes that she gave birth to a healthy girl before an audience of onlookers, as was common in Versailles to prevent the substitution of children, but that she sickened soon afterwards. He understood that neither she nor the child survived the first month. They said the king was heartbroken. It was said that he was there for her last breath, and that he wept, when he saw what he had done to his darling.

Now Charles knows what Marie is telling him, though; he is quick enough for that at least. Given her daughter Thérèse's age and name, it is clear the child survived after all, and was smuggled to Paris for safekeeping. Thérèse is not Marie's by birth. And is Françoise a child of the king too? They have the look of sisters. How many illegitimate children, Charles wonders, does the king have concealed around the capital? Yet how Marie has protected the girls here; what a home she has made for them! Charles feels himself deeply moved by her kindness; almost unbalanced by it.

'You didn't, then, conceive them by— I thought . . . I had assumed you must have had many lovers,' Charles finds himself admitting. It shocks him, how violently grateful he feels that she has not. How dare he feel so! Was he truly that envious, when it was none of his business?

'Only the one. Bonenfant, who was executed.'

'And you were never a spy?'

'No,' she says. 'It is my mother who has the taste for intrigue. She has found a life in England, where I believe she is quite an asset for France, but I have no stomach for it. Did you think I was a spy?'

'Maybe,' he replies. 'People talk, and I listened, God forgive me. Do you forgive me?'

She nods, almost amused, that he might think he needs forgiveness. But her story still won't come somehow: it is like trying to make yourself sick on purpose.

'You are like Madame de Maintenon, back when she was a governess,' Charles says, as if to help her. 'Who looked after the king and Athénaïs's children in that house in the Rue de Vaugirard. That is the truth, am I right? That was the deal that allowed you to return to Paris. Secretly bringing up illegitimate children is the service that you render to the Crown.'

'Yes, I – yes.' Marie falters, so used to keeping silent that speaking *yes* aloud feels like a betrayal of her daughters; a disowning. For she loves them dearly: her glorious, clever, kind, funny girls. And she empathizes, almost too much, with their poor mothers – just the thought of what they went through, no! When she shuts her eyes, droplets of light and blood stream beneath her lids. But she realizes, too, how much she wants Charles to know the story: an untold tale is such a heavy thing to carry. 'I gave birth to Judith,' she tells him. 'But the others are adopted.'

'So you have brought up Françoise and Thérèse discreetly for the king. They are his own – of royal descent – but they do not know.'

She nods. 'But *he* knows,' she adds, her face all screwed up with it.

'He knows,' Charles repeats. He breathes in and out through his nostrils. 'Yes, yes, I see. It is quite the tale of "Donkey-Skin"! Thérèse is his daughter. His Thérèse come back.' She nods again. 'Is there more?' he asks her. 'I mean, if you want to tell me, of course.'

'Athénaïs,' she blurts. 'They told me she was sus-pected of poisoning the first Thérèse with a piece of fruit. A pear. Out of jealousy, for her youth and beauty. One of those fat half-blush pears from the kitchen garden, her favourites – well, everybody's favourites. She brought a silver bowl of them to the girl's child-bed. That's why he wanted my Thérèse brought up in Paris. My little Françoise later too, when he got some maid pregnant. He was afraid of what Athénaïs might do to them.'

'Oh God, Marie.'

'I wish him ringworm, the plague and a broken neck,' she hisses. 'They should cut his fucking DICK off!'

Screwing up the letter, she hurls it in the fire where the little fleur-de-lis blackens, shrivels, then is gone.

'Shall I tell them to fuck off, then?' Charles asks, almost giddily, straightening himself.

'Yes please, especially if you could rephrase that in the style of an immortal of the Académie Française,' she says, and then she laughs, and he does too, in delight that she has laughed.

'They are disgusting people,' he observes. 'I thought we were making a Heaven, but it is Hell that's hung with so many mirrors. Well of course then, your Thérèse must not go. She will not go. I will let them know as much. You are their mother, Marie, whatever the circumstances of their birth, and you are a wonderful, loving mother. What will the king do? Have us read "Donkey-Skin" out to the chief of police? Stop your allowance? We shall manage.' But he has overstepped himself there. He thanks God she doesn't seem to notice, as he trots off quickly down the stairs.

She watches him through the window, leaning into the carriage to speak. He is saying something about how, given his historic relation to the household, they feel it might not be entirely appropriate for the king and Thérèse to meet in such a manner as might create misguided speculation or gossip, or reach Athénaïs or Madame Maintenon's attention. When he returns, the white horses have been whipped into motion. The carriage has gone, for now. Her composure has returned a little. 'Thank you, Charles,' she says, giving the words their full weight. 'I'm glad you know.'

'You can rely on me to keep your secret, of course, completely – I mean, I hope that much is obvious.'

'I know. Do you think he will lock me up in a tower again?' Marie asks, with a strange levity. For she feels, in this moment, terrifyingly free – as if her ending, after all, is still unwritten.

'The Sun King's image has been badly tarnished of late, he cannot afford a further scandal, and his new mistress Maintenon is determined to refashion him as some kind of exemplar of Christian kingship. I have a feeling he may be merciful.'

'Mercy!' she exclaims. 'I don't know why but the word always chills me. To exist within his gift.'

'You're right,' Charles says. 'I misspoke. I mean only that the king might be reminded of his conscience for once. What now? Should I go?' But she does not nod. He begins to pick up icicles of glass off the floor. A crimson petal pools on his fingertip.

'Please don't,' she says. 'You'll hurt yourself.'

'I want to,' he says, and he begins to cry, silently, shuddering. It is his turn now, it seems. He tries to stand. They are very close; touching close. He wishes he could kiss her but he must not kiss her, but still, he leans towards her, somehow, drawn, and finds his forehead rests against hers for a moment. Like her head is the door. 'I am in love with you,' he mumbles. And then: 'I'm sorry, I'm so sorry.'

'I might have nits,' she says. Why does she say this? Because she is scared. Because she has wanted, so long, to make herself untouchable.

231

'I don't mind that, my boys always seem to have them,' he replies, and Marie kisses him, just for a second, on the lips. A friendly kiss, he thinks, a little hesitant peck, which is enough. Which should be more than enough. It is very generous of her, to give him such a blessing. 'I feel like a frog,' he quips, immediately aware how grotesque this joke has made him – positively inviting her to make comparison between his visage and a frog's – and he backs away, clumsily, and tries to wipe his eyes with his wrists.

'But I don't want you to change, Charles,' she says.

'I should go,' he tells her. 'Thank you, Marie, for everything, and I apologize. That was . . . it was improper of me. I—' He reaches here for some appropriate formulation. Where's a quote from Racine when you need one? He can only think of 'Love is not a fire to be shut up in the soul' which is the last quote that he needs right now. Shut up, soul! Please shut up! Haha.

'What a Parnassus this was, madame,' he manages, instead. 'I mean to say, your salons will be remembered in the history books as a high point in the civilization of France. I need you to know that I admire you terribly.'

'But I thought that you were in love with me,' she says then, deciding. Her soft face is tilted up at him – full lips, her little chin – her eyes warm brown like fur, and he can see her, he realizes. He can see the her inside herself, and she can see him back.

'What?' Charles says, his whole face braced in an ugly grimace, because he does not dare to hope. If he has misunderstood this then he would rather die.

'I was so happy to hear it,' Marie tells him. 'Because, although I am not free to marry, it is my wish that you might allow me to love you in return.'

'Please,' he says. 'Is this real?'

The answer is a quick nod, then a kiss with her real mouth, the flesh and blood of it. She kisses him properly this time, in the French manner, and they kiss and kiss – the exquisite relief of it! If there's such a thing as a kiss of true love, then we must declare that this is one of them: this moment in which their whole life trembles, like the world reflected in a drop of dew.

25. The Tale of the Enchanted Letter

But wait – stay just a little longer by the fire. Perhaps you thought this Mother Goose might end her story here, but though it's true that too much further and we'll follow these salonnières into their graves, I still have one more tale I want to tell.

It is a couple of months later. Autumn has come, bringing its blood-drop berries, its acorns and walnuts, its spiders' webs. The sap is falling, as the trees draw their nutrients back inside, readying themselves for their long, enchanted sleep, whilst their leaves – which in their youth were simply green – each seem to become unique, in their last hours: blotched, spotted, blush-tipped, pocked, crinkled; the colours of gingerbread, bearskin, pumpkin, ram's fur, porridge, a bloodstained key.

Such colours can only be glimpsed at a distance by Henriette-Julie de Murat, who watches the distant trees tussle from her small stone room in the Château de Loches, the huge ninth-century castle in the Loire Valley that Louis XIV uses as a state prison. Her view is limited to one tiny window. At night she can hear the distant howl of wolves; in the morning the first rays of light break over the horizon like spun straw.

Without a wig, Henriette's black hair is tied back in a simple style; her dress is plain. 'Good morning, sire,' she greets the robin who often sits on her windowsill in the morning, tempted by the trail of crumbs she leaves between the bars. Today he carries some squirming catch. She calls him Bleakthought. Sometimes, now, Bleakthought even hops on to her desk as she writes her correspondence, seeming to glance up at her: such small soft feathers; such sharp black eyes. 'Is that a worm in your beak or are you just pleased to see me?' Henriette asks, and she feels gratified with herself, for a moment.

This is how she uses up her wit these days. This is how bored she is.

Still, nobody hits her in the Château de Loches. They allow her access to the library so she reads a great many books; she writes poetry and is working on a ghost story and a fairy tale called 'Le Roi Porc'; she wanks, occasionally. She must attend chapel, so has had a great deal of time to contemplate her faith, and has come to the realization – after much thought – that, after all, she has none.

And at least they are permitted to receive letters. When they arrive each morning, Henriette likes to leave them on the side for a while, to savour the anticipation, and then she opens and reads them with great, slow care, imagining them spoken aloud in her friends' voices. One has arrived this dawn, she sees, from Madame d'Aulnoy. Lovely Marie. She opens it, now.

Dear Henriette,

I am writing to you from Paris, where all is well. In my last letter I believe I told you that Charles and I have now reached an understanding. Well, though we still keep to our two households — as is appropriate, given my married status — I am pleased to say we see each other daily. Often, we visit the theatre, walk in the Tuileries, or attend his cousin Télésille's new salon — for she has inherited the Saturday Club from her friend Mademoiselle de Scudéry — and our sons and daughters make a very merry picture when we dine at the weekend together. Though my income has recently been greatly reduced due to the loss of a patron, I have sold some of my gold and silver plate for a fair price, and I know that I am still fortunate in my position — for after all, even the king has had to melt down his plate lately, to fund his wars.

I am certain that Télésille must write to you twice daily. Perhaps you have been in correspondence too with Charlotte-Rose? I am pleased to say that she seems to have settled in contentedly at the abbey of Gercy-en-Brie, working in the kitchen garden (she communicates to me proudly about the size of her turnips!) and penning more great literature, of course. Those sisters seem to have cultivated their own little isle of quiet pleasures. She tells me too that she is working on a memoir, Pensées chrétiennes de défunte de Mlle de La Force.

But there are other friends from my salon who I am very aware that you must miss. Charles quoted the playwright Racine to me the other day — you know what a memory Charles has for quotation — and I thought that I might share these words with you in this letter, whilst imploring you not to give up hope of seeing beloved ones again:

*'Love is not a fire to be shut up in a soul. Everything betrays
us: voice, silence, eyes; half-covered fires burn all the brighter.'*
Is there a candle in your room, my friend?

With great affection,
Marie d'Aulnoy

The answer is yes, there is a wax candle on Henriette's
desk. She looks at the candle. 'Half-covered fires burn all
the brighter,' she says aloud. 'Half-covered fires burn
all the brighter.'

And a vivid, shaky thought passes over her; a smile
begins to play on her lips.

Having lit the candle, Henriette holds the letter over
its dancing flame, to see a second text slowly emerge
beneath Marie's – as if by some enchantment – darkening
against the illuminated paper, scrawled in lemon juice:

Dear Henriette,

*They cannot expect me to live without the love of my life. I
cannot stop thinking about you, so I simply refuse to do so.
With Marie's assistance, I have bribed a chambermaid who
tonight will deliver a parcel to you that contains men's clothing.
Once you are dressed in it, she will help you escape through the
back gates, where you shall find me waiting impatiently upon
my horse. I hope you shall forgive the choice of clothes – you see,
I have a fancy, sometimes, that you might be my Prince, for I
am, as always,*

Your Princess

Is Henriette crying, do you think, or laughing? Sometimes it's hard to tell. And I cannot quite promise happy ever after – not even an old storyteller such as I.

But this I swear: she is happy now. She is so happy now.

Author's Note

This novel is inspired by the real adventures of 'the Modern Fairies' of the late seventeenth century who shaped fairy tales as we know them. It is also a creative engagement with the brilliant tales that they wrote. I first learnt about these contes de fées through the work of Marina Warner, Jack Zipes and Angela Carter, all of whom I highly recommend for further reading. I have taken many liberties in the service of a good story – from speculating wildly about the sex lives of the salonnières to playing extremely loose with the chronology – though I must tell you, an almost unbelievable amount of this is true.

Acknowledgements

Thanks are due to my incredible agents, whose belief in this book meant so much to me: Jenny Hewson in the UK and Lucy Carson in the US. To Helen Garnons-Williams and Lauren Wein, the editorial dream-team, for making the whole process such a pleasure and your impeccable notes. Thanks also to Ella Harold, Amy Guay, and Sarah-Jane Forder for copy-editing.

I am always grateful for the support of my mum and my children, Gruff and Cate. And a special mention for my in-laws, John and Helen, who accompanied us around Paris and Versailles on a very hot half-term holiday.

This book is dedicated to Richard on our twentieth wedding anniversary, with love always.

Acknowledgements